Praise
Brian Morela

"Witchcraft, sacrifices, an abandoned house and a thing that has hungered for decades set the stage for this must-read expedition to *The Witching House*."
—**John Everson,** author of *NightWhere* and *Violet Eyes*

"Sometimes a horror reader just wants an action packed story...just pulse pounding, shrieking monster terror. Moreland delivers exactly that with *They Stalk The Night*. Everything I love is wrapped up in a story perfect for a dark wintry night." —**Roxanne M., Netgalley**

"*Tomb of Gods* completely knocked me out from beginning to end, with some of the sequences so unrelentingly fast moving it was impossible to put down…the mythology explored in the second half of the story is simply outstanding…an absolute delight."
—**Tony's Top 10 Horror Novels of 2020, HorrorDNA.coms**

"*Tomb of Gods* is fantastically imaginative, darkly fun, and horrifically astounding." —**Deadhead Reviews**

"*The Devil's Woods* is an awesome horror novel, filled with nerve-wracking suspense and thrilling action!"
—**Jeff Strand,** author of *Wolf Hunt*

"Brian Moreland's fiction is taut and spellbinding, often blending varied themes to form a dark genre very much his own."
—**Greg F. Gifune,** author of *The Bleeding Season*

Books by Brian Moreland:

Shadows in the Mist
The Devil's Woods
The Witching House
The Seekers
Darkness Rising
Tomb of Gods
Savage Island
They Stalk the Night

THE WITCHING HOUSE

Brian Moreland

RED MONSTER BOOKS

The Witching House

Published June 2025 by Red Monster Books

2nd Edition, Printed in the U.S.A.

This book is a work of fiction. The names, characters, places, and incidents are products of the writer's imagination or have been used fictitiously and are not to be construed as real. Any resemblance to persons, living or dead, actual events, locale or organizations is entirely coincidental.

The Girl from the Blood Coven and *The Witching House* were originally published as eBooks by Samhain Publishing July 2013. Both stories were also included in a paperback collection: *Blood Sacrifices: Four Tales of Terror*, published by Samhain Publishing April 2016. Published February 2017 by Rising Horse Books.

Cover design: Brian Moreland
stone house image © chiakto - Fotolia.com

ISBN: 978-0-9986846-1-1

To my wonderful nieces, Saxon and Ally.

Follow your dreams.

THE GIRL FROM THE BLOOD COVEN

Short Story Prequel to *The Witching House*

June 21, 1972

As Sheriff Travis Keagan drove through the pine country of East Texas, he had two things on his mind: drinking a cold beer and watching the second half of the Rangers baseball game. On the radio, the announcer said it was top of the fifth and the Yankees were winning five to three.

"Come on, Rangers." Sheriff Keagan felt absolutely beat and needed his team to lift his spirits. It was the end of another long, hot and balmy summer day of dealing with traffic accidents, drunken domestic disputes and escorting a wife beater to the county jail. Now the shadows of dusk were gathering in the forest, and judging by the flickering clouds, a stormy night was fast approaching.

A woman's voice squawked on the CB radio. "Dispatch to Sheriff. Over."

Sheriff Keagan sighed and picked up the microphone. "Yes, Candice. Over."

"Earl Potter called and claims he saw the ghost of a girl cross through his pasture. Says she spooked his horses."

"Ghost…" Keagan chuckled, shaking his head. "Last week it was flying saucers. Did he sound drunk?"

Candice laughed. "Like he always does. Over."

"Tell Earl he needs to lay off the moonshine and go to bed. I'm calling it a night. Have a wonderful evening, Candice. I'll be at the Armadillo if you need me. Over and out." Keagan parked his police car in the gravel lot of the Lazy Armadillo. The roadhouse and connecting gas station were isolated on a wooded road just outside of the small town of Buck Horn. Inside the restaurant, the jukebox was playing a Willie Nelson song. A half-dozen townspeople acknowledged the sheriff as he entered the bar. He knew everyone here by name, where they lived, where they worked and their nighttime habits. He knew that Dale and Judy in the corner booth were cheating on their spouses. At another table, Tommy Green was studying to be a lawyer so he didn't have to end up selling cars his whole life like his pops. And the sheriff knew that the Kincaid brothers, who were casually playing pool, would later get drunk and start throwing fists at one another. Just a typical night at the Armadillo.

Taking off his cowboy hat, Keagan sat at his favorite bar stool, where he had a perfect view of the Rangers game on the TV. "Damn, Yanks scored again?"

Sheila, the sexiest redheaded bartender in the county, put a frosty mug in front of Keagan. "Rangers' pitching is terrible tonight."

"Their bats aren't hitting squat either," Keagan said.

She pulled out her order pad. "Your usual tonight, Sheriff?"

"Nah, I'm in the mood for a steak. Tell Jorge to burn it."

Sheila leaned against the bar. "You know all that red

meat isn't good for your colon." The student nurse was always looking after his health. "How about the grilled catfish with some stir-fried veggies? You'll thank me twenty years from now."

"Fine. But you're not talking me out of the pecan pie."

"Maybe I'll have a slice with you." She winked.

Keagan's cheeks flushed and he felt warm all over. Since his wife left him a few years back, moving to Houston with their daughter, he missed having a woman care about him. He admired Sheila as she delivered his order to the kitchen. If the college girl wasn't half his age, he'd ask her out in a heartbeat.

On the TV, the Rangers hit a homer with two men on base, tying the game.

Keagan cheered and waved the runners around the bases. He raised his beer in celebration and was about to drink when he heard a commotion behind him.

A man shouted, "Holy shit!"

Keagan spun around in his seat.

Standing in the front doorway was a young woman covered head to toe in blood. Her soaked nightgown clung to her body. She walked into the restaurant, stiff and grimacing, as if her bare feet were walking on glass. The girl's face was a mask of solid red and her eyes were wide with terror. She stretched out an arm. "Help me…"

Keagan reached her first and she collapsed in his arms. She was trembling.

So much blood. It covered his hands and stained his uniform.

A crowd of onlookers gathered around, and the sheriff shouted, "Everyone stay back. Sheila, call for an ambulance. And somebody get her some water." Keagan walked the girl to a booth and sat her down. He examined her exposed skin for bleeding wounds, but found none. It looked as if someone had dumped buckets of dark red paint over her head. Her long hair was littered with leaves and pine needles. Her gown was slashed across the chest and he could see part of one of her breasts. "Are you hurt anywhere?"

The girl looked at him, her lips quivering, and made a croaking sound.

The waitress gave her a glass of water.

As the girl drank, Keagan said, "You're going to be okay. You're safe now. An ambulance will be here soon. My name is Sheriff Keagan. Can you tell me what happened?"

"Dead..." she managed. "They're all dead."

* * *

At the hospital, Sheriff Keagan paced the hall, eager for some answers. His two night-shift deputies, Pete Stubbs and Big Mike Jablonski, were standing beside the door to the room where the girl was being treated. When a doctor in scrubs finally came out, Keagan rushed to him. "How is she?"

"Stable."

"What's the status on her wounds?"

"Oddly, the girl has no wounds. Just a few bruises and scrapes on her feet."

"Then where did all that blood come from?"

"That's for you to find out, Sheriff. But it wasn't hers. I did get one thing out of your mystery girl. Her name is

Abigail. Oh, and she's definitely on some kind of drugs, and not the prescription kind either." The doctor nodded toward the door. "She's awake if you want to talk to her."

Keagan entered the private room and closed the door. He said softly, "Hey, Abigail, how are you?"

The girl was sitting against a pillow on her bed. She had been cleaned up. Her pale skin still had pink marks from being scrubbed. Her damp black hair hung over her face and shoulders. At first Abigail looked catatonic; then her eyes followed the sheriff as he rounded the bed and sat in a chair. She cowered away from him.

"It's okay," he soothed. "You're safe with me."

The girl stared at him with haunted blue eyes. Her dilated pupils were almost as wide as her irises. She looked to be around twenty-five. Definitely not a native to Buck Horn. Keagan knew everyone in town.

"I know you've been through a lot, miss, but I need to ask you some questions so we can find your family. Can you talk to me?"

She teared up as she nodded.

He pulled out a pen and notepad. "What's your last name?"

"Blackwood."

"Abigail Blackwood," he wrote, offering a comforting smile. "You can call me Travis. Now, can you tell me what happened?"

Her lips trembled as she tried to form the words. "We… we were all inside our house." She sniffled and wiped a tear off her cheek. "We were just singing and dancing and then it attacked us."

"What? An animal?"

"I don't know. Something in the house. Everybody started screaming. Then there was all this blood and my brothers and sisters were…" She wiped away more tears.

"Did you see what was attacking them?"

Abigail shook her head. "It was too dark. All the power had shut off. I just ran."

"I need to go to your house. What's the address?"

"The Blevins House off Copper Creek Road."

Keagan felt a burning in his stomach. "The hippy commune?"

Abigail said, "We preferred to call our family a coven."

A God-fearing Christian, Keagan had trouble even writing the word coven in his notes. He had known enough about the Blevins House to stay away from it. Set far back in the woods, the commune was run by a witch named Lenora Ravenmoon Blevins. She had a reputation for giving the people in town a hard time. Lenora was always taking in strays, mostly teenage runaways and college dropouts. Keagan had busted a few of them for possession of marijuana and psychedelic drugs. The members of the Blevins commune represented everything Keagan hated about hippies. Abigail certainly fit the description of a flower child. Knowing that she was also a witch made Keagan uncomfortable.

"How many people were in your group?"

"Twenty-five of us."

"How many men?"

"Five. The rest were women and children."

"Anyone else escape?"

She shook her head.

Keagan sighed, trying to think of what kind of animal

could attack an entire house of men and women. Abigail's story sounded hard to swallow. Keagan knew plenty of religious groups in these woods who didn't like having witches for neighbors.

"Did you hear any gunshots?" he asked.

"No, just screams."

"Is it possible you were attacked by a group of men?"

"No, it definitely wasn't human."

The burning sensation in Keagan's stomach spread to his chest. "One last question. Were you doing drugs earlier tonight?"

Abigail shook her head no, but Keagan could tell by the twitch in her face as she averted his gaze that she was lying.

The sheriff stepped back into the hallway and huddled his deputies. To the six-foot-four man, Keagan said, "Big Mike, guard this door and don't let Abigail leave. As soon as the doctor releases her, take her to the station. She's a possible suspect."

"Is she under arrest?"

"Not yet." To the smaller deputy, Keagan said, "Pete, you're coming with me."

"Where are we going, Sheriff?"

"The Blevins House."

* * *

Driving away from the hospital, Keagan radioed Candice at the station and explained where they were going.

She responded, "Want me to call in some backup?

Over."

"Hold off. Pete and I are going to investigate the matter first. Over."

"Be careful. Over."

"Roger and out."

No use waking up half the police in the county if it turned out Abigail had suffered a bad LSD trip and imagined the attack. Keagan couldn't explain all the blood that had covered her body. Although, he had heard reports from some of the neighboring ranchers that the Blevins witches were performing blood sacrifices. Maybe some of the hippies pulled a prank on Abigail and dumped goat's blood all over her.

The last thing on earth Keagan wanted to do tonight was drive out to the Blevins House. It was set far back on two hundred acres of thick forest land. He'd heard plenty of rumors about the commune, but had never actually gone there. The Blevins witches were strange folk, but for the most part they had kept to themselves.

Lightning crackled in the night sky. The car's windshield wipers fought against torrents of rain as Keagan sped down a narrow dirt road between two walls of trees.

He could tell by the way Pete gripped his door that he was close to shitting bricks.

"Hopefully this is just a girl's wild imagination," Keagan said.

"I knew something bad would eventually happen at that house," Pete said.

"How so?"

"'Cause them witches are devil worshippers. And when you mess with the devil, it can only end up bad."

The road opened up to a driveway full of VW vans and old cars. Keagan parked, but left the engine running. They remained seated in the car for a moment. The headlights shone on a rock house that towered three stories. All the windows were dark. Every few seconds, lightning flashed, illuminating the pitched roof. The thunder that followed made Pete jerk in his seat.

"Damn, I hate storms," he said.

The wipers continued to squeak across the windshield. Rain thumped on the car's roof.

Keagan studied the gloomy woods that surrounded the house. He kept a stone face, but inside his nerves were bouncing. "All right, let's check things out."

The sheriff and deputy switched on their flashlights and stepped out of the car. Keagan unsnapped his holster and kept his hand on the butt of his pistol as he approached the house with Pete flanking his left side. Their beams reflected in the windows. Rainwater dribbled down the glass, making it damned hard to see inside.

Keagan stepped up to the front door and knocked. The door opened an inch. He knocked again. "Hello?" When no one answered, he pushed the door open wide. "Police! Anybody home?" His voice echoed off the cobblestone floor in the foyer. A dark hallway stretched straight ahead. To his right and left were two living areas. The walls were covered in colorful hippy art: peace signs, rainbow buses and marijuana leafs. On one wall, he spotted an arc of blood splatter.

Keagan drew his pistol and entered. He was immediately hit by a stench that was undeniably death—a mix of blood, urine and evacuated bowels. In the den to his right, the floor was covered in feathers. The cushions on a couch had been torn to shreds. In the center of the room a man lay face down in the feathers. His head had been smashed in like a melon.

"Pete, we got a body."

His deputy stepped up beside him. "Oh, God..." He covered his mouth and puked in a corner.

Keagan didn't blame the rookie. This was his first corpse. "Pull yourself together and stay with me." The sheriff walked forward, more on edge than before. The entry into the next room was a beaded doorway. All he could see between the streamers was pitch darkness. The killer could be hiding inside that void. Keagan's heart quickened. The beads rattled as he pushed them aside. He jerked his beam left, catching a bloody handprint on the wall. He followed a trail of blood smears past a long dining table that was still covered with plates and bowls of food. A bottle of wine had tipped over, spilling crimson liquid all over the rug. Hippy shit everywhere--bongs and pipes and ashtrays filled to the brim with cigarettes and ash.

They found a second body in the kitchen—a woman with several knives in her chest. When Keagan moved his light up to see her face, he found only the bloody stump of her neck.

Pete whispered, "Christ almighty, where's her head?"

Keagan signaled to keep hush. He passed through the kitchen, checking the countertops and sink, but didn't see the woman's severed head anywhere. The other end of the kitchen led into a hallway. The smell coming from the darkness ahead was so horrendous it pushed his gag reflex. He glanced back at Pete. The young deputy was wide-eyed with terror, but keeping pace.

Keagan entered a den with a stone floor that was sticky to his boots. His jaw dropped as he panned his flashlight around the room. The floor and walls were decorated in pagan symbols. Some kind of ceremonial room. In the center of a giant circle on the floor was a bowl of animal skulls and various bones.

Pete said, "I knew they were devil worshippers."

There was blood everywhere, pooled on the floor in multiple places, spattered across the walls, but no bodies. Keagan observed another detail that bothered him. Scattered across the floor were dirt clods and broken roots. Ahead something slammed, startling both men. The sheriff and deputy rushed into the next room—an enclosed patio with screen walls. The noise turned out to be the storm slamming an open back door against the house.

* * *

On the ride back to the police station, Big Mike Jablonski fumbled with the radio dial until he landed on Merle Haggard singing "I'm a Lonesome Fugitive."

"You like country music?" Big Mike asked the girl.

Abigail Blackwood was sitting in the backseat, a silhouette against the storm light from the back window. She hadn't said a word since he walked her out of the hospital. The doctor had given her a tight jumpsuit to wear. The hippy girl was a looker. Youthful face, skinny body, perky tits. The fact that she was a witch made the fantasy that played in Big Mike's mind all the more taboo.

He passed the forest road that led to the Blevins House

and wondered how the sheriff and Pete were doing.

Sheriff Keagan's frantic voice suddenly squawked on the CB. "Big Mike, you there? Over."

The deputy shut off the music and grabbed his mic. "Roger, Sheriff. Over."

"What's your twenty?"

"Halfway to the station. Over."

"When you get there, lock the suspect in a cell. Copy?"

"Roger. Everything all right, Sheriff?"

"Just follow orders. Out."

Damn, his sexy little witch was going behind bars. Big Mike looked in the rearview mirror and couldn't see Abigail. He glanced over his shoulder. She was lying across the backseat.

He turned the radio back on and was assaulted by ear-piercing static. He surfed the dials, but got nothing but more static. Strange. Buck Horn always picked up at least four radio stations. Then he heard singing. Only it was coming from the backseat. A lilting song in a language Big Mike had never heard before. He whirled in his seat.

Abigail sat up suddenly. Her eyes were rolled back to whites.

* * *

Sheriff Keagan and Pete stood by the car in front of the house. After talking to Big Mike, Keagan radioed Candice. "We need backup at the Blevins House and lots of it." He named off the nearby towns in which to call. The sheriff had seen enough to know this was a job for a county-wide task force. Whoever murdered twenty-plus people was not someone Keagan wanted to face in a dark house with just one inexperienced deputy.

The rain continued to drench them. Water dripped over the brim of Keagan's cowboy hat and soaked his uniform. He was cold and miserable as he watched the house.

"Who do you think did all that?" Pete asked, visibly traumatized.

Keagan shook his head. "Someone with a sick mind. Possibly multiple killers." He thought of the Charlie Manson Family and all the bizarre killings they had committed in California. The blood on the walls of this house reminded him of the crime photos that had been published from the Manson case. Hippies doing all those mind-altering drugs. It was only a matter of time before somebody flipped out and went on a killing spree.

A siren wailed in the distance. Flashing red and blue lights approached quickly down the long dirt road. Good, someone had already responded to the call. The sheriff and deputy rounded their vehicle to greet the officer.

The police car barreled into the driveway and kept coming toward them at high speed.

"Shit, move!" Keagan dove out of the car's path and rolled across wet grass. He looked back to see the squad car crush Pete against the sheriff's car with a deafening crash. The two vehicles slid several feet and smashed into a tree.

"Oh, Christ!" Keagan rushed to the tangled police cars.

From the chest down, Pete Stubbs was pinned between the grill and side door. His face was bloody and full of glass, his eyes wide and lifeless.

Keagan felt an overwhelming rush of grief and anger. He hurried around to the driver's side to see what goddamned idiot had failed to hit the brakes. He opened the driver's door and Big Mike fell halfway out. His eyes were missing.

The sheriff backed away from the car, stunned. As the rain poured down in heavy cords, he tried to make sense of what the hell just happened. And then he remembered Abigail had been riding in back. He opened the back door of Big Mike's car and found the seat empty. On the opposite side, the passenger door hung open.

Keagan looked up in time to see the girl run into the house. "Fuck!" He pulled out his pistol and ran to the front door. "Abigail, come back out here!" He entered the foyer, swishing his beam, pistol cocked and ready to shoot the girl if she attacked. How she killed Big Mike and all these people Keagan couldn't fathom. The girl was maybe ninety pounds wet. "Abigail, turn yourself in. It's the best way out of this."

He glanced back outside. Where were his reinforcements?

From down the hall, the girl started singing in a strange language. *"Dheannain sùgradh an àm dùsgaidh…'N àm na siùil a bhith 'gam pasgadh…"*

Keagan followed her voice until he reached a wide stairway at the center of the house. She continued to croon loudly from above, *"Di-Luain an dèidh Di-dòmhnaich… Dh'fhalbh sinn le Seonaid a Aircaibh…"*

He raised his flashlight beam up the muddy stairs. Abigail was standing on the second floor railing.

"Freeze!" Keagan aimed his pistol.

She smiled as she sang and put a noose around her neck. The girl leaped. Keagan stepped back as she fell toward him. Halfway down, the rope snapped her neck. Her body swung like a pendulum.

Keagan fell back against the wall. He'd seen plenty of dead bodies, but never had he watched someone die.

Abigail Blackwood kept spinning in a circle, her eyes and tongue bulging out. He grabbed her ankle and stopped her motion. Feeling numb, Keagan walked back to the front door and stood at the threshold. Outside, the storm continued to flash and rumble over the pine forest. The driveway was empty except for the two police cars where Big Mike and Pete remained dead.

"Christ, what a night." Keagan heard a new sound coming from *inside* the house. He stepped back into the hall. Somewhere in the darkness someone was crying. Was Abigail still alive? He walked back to her hanging body. Her blank eyes stared down at him. Her face was already turning blue. He grabbed her dangling arm and checked her pulse. Definitely dead.

The sobbing started up again.

His pistol aimed at the impenetrable blackness, the sheriff followed the hall until he was back inside the kitchen. The crying seemed to be coming from the pantry. He opened it and found a small corridor that ended at a partially open door. The floor and walls were covered in dirt, broken roots and smears of blood.

The cry was much louder now. A child's voice.

Keagan opened the door. A set of blood-stained steps led down into a cellar. His claustrophobia kicked in, constricting his breath. He hated cellars. *Go back outside,* his inner voice urged. *Let someone else go down there.*

No, he was the sheriff of this county, he reminded himself, and a child was crying for help.

Keagan tried the light switch, but the power was dead. “Shit!” He descended the stairs until his boots sank in moist black soil. He rounded the staircase to find a cavernous darkness of unknown depth. The one wall he could see was lined with shelves stored with jars of fruit preserves and pickled pigs’ feet. He followed the sobs that sounded like a boy’s cry. The stink of death was heavy in the air, burning Keagan’s nostrils. As he got twenty feet under the house, the crying stopped. “Where are you, son?” He spun in a circle and his light caught movement. “There you are.” He spotlighted a red-faced boy sucking his thumb.

Keagan recognized Otis Blevins. The six-year-old was the only retarded boy in Buck Horn. “Everything’s going to be okay, Otis. I’m going to get you out of here.” As the sheriff walked toward him, the flashlight illuminated something behind the boy that made Keagan freeze. Jutting up from the soil, impaled on sticks, were a dozen decapitated heads. The missing members of the coven.

Otis’s eyes got wide and he backed into the maze of the killer’s trophies.

A loud cracking noise echoed behind Keagan. He whirled with the flashlight and gasped, “Oh, Jesus…” when he saw the Blevins House killer.

* * *

An hour later, the police reinforcements finally made their way down to the cellar. They rescued little Otis

Blevins. The boy cried for his mama as they took him upstairs. The half-dozen cops who searched the cellar couldn't believe what was down here. Among a bizarre collection of witches' heads, they found Sheriff Keagan's head mounted on a stick.

✱✱✱

"White Ceremonial Magic is, by the terms of its
definition, an attempt to communicate with Good Spirits
for a good, or at least an innocent, purpose.
Black Magic is the attempt to communicate with
Evil Spirits for evil purposes."

—Arthur Edward Waite, *The Book of Black Magic,*
originally published in 1898

THE WITCHING HOUSE

Prologue

Present day

The house that ate people stood within a coven of pine trees like an ancient god being worshipped. The high branches touched its shingled roof with reverence. Towering three stories, the rock house was far from being a flawless god. The moss-covered stones that cobbled its walls were pocked from years of rot and abandon. Fungus and creeper vines had spread across its facade, leafy tentacles invading cracks where boards covered the windows. The glass within their frames had long ago shattered.

The Old Blevins House, as it came to be called, was set miles deep within the East Texas forest and rumored to be haunted. The stone dwelling became a backwoods legend spoken over campfires and around beers at the roadhouse in Buck Horn, referring to it as "that house in the woods." If anyone foolishly talked about ghosts or witchery, they were sure to spit the ground and cross themselves. Deer hunters wouldn't dare hunt these parts. The deer wouldn't come here either.

Otis Blevins, the caretaker of the property, knew all the house's secrets because he had witnessed his family's bloody massacre as a child. Now, decades later, the house often spoke to him in whispers and played violent memories inside his head. Some folk called Otis Blevins crazy, but he wasn't. He just had a special bond with this house that ran deep as blood.

At age forty-seven, Otis now lived on a pig farm ten miles away but still looked after the stone house. On this dewy morning, he checked the front door to make sure it was still locked. The padlock was badly rusted. He made a mental note to stop by the hardware store and buy a new one. As the caretaker walked the perimeter, he noticed that some of the symbols painted on the clapboards had smeared after last night's storm. He shook his head. East Texas got too much rain this time of year.

Otis pulled a paintbrush out of a mason jar of hog's blood and repainted a symbol of a triangle with stick-figure arms and legs. He heard scratching from the opposite side of the clapboards—something angry clawed at him from within the house. Whistling, Otis walked around the corner. The scraping nails followed him as he painted the same symbol on every boarded window. The scrapes turned to pounding. The house was in a foul mood this morning. Or maybe just hungry. The caretaker ignored the incessant knocks against the wood and performed the tasks that the house had given him.

When he was done, Otis returned to his truck. In the back, a large hog was pacing in a cage, making all sorts of grunting noises.

"Easy there, girl." Otis opened the cage and snapped a leash on Bessie's collar. The sow hopped off the truck and snorted against Otis's leg. He patted her pink head and then walked her to the back of the house where a long chain lay coiled on the ground. He was mighty upset that it was Bessie's turn. Otis loved this pig. The house reminded him that he had alternatives, if he was willing.

The caretaker hooked the chain to the sow's collar and backed away. Tearing up, Otis sat in an old rocker and chewed a wad of tobacco as he waited. Not long after, the chain began to uncoil and went taut. The pig squealed and struggled to run as she was dragged into a dark hole near the house.

Otis left after that. He hated the sounds the house made when it fed.

Part One

The Ghost Squad

1

"Dead roads are bad omens," Sarah Donovan's grandmother used to say when Sarah was a little girl and her family traveled down a road littered with road kill. "You'll find nothing good at the end of a dead road."

Today, while riding through the backwoods of East Texas with her new boyfriend, Dean, and another couple, Sarah had counted a dead coyote, two mutilated armadillos, what might have been a possum, and buzzards feasting on a deer carcass. The carrion eaters took flight as the white Range Rover passed them and wound its way through the cloying pines.

Sarah's nana, who was in to everything New Age, had preached that the universe always gives you signs if you watch for them.

Is this road trying to warn me? Sarah wondered. She looked at her boyfriend. *Does this mean our relationship is doomed?*

Dean seemed oblivious to the signs all around them. As he and his friends, Casey and Meg Ackerman, passed around a thermos of coffee and talked over strategy, Sarah remained quiet in the front passenger seat. Since they had left Dallas at dawn, she had seen a few truck stops and small towns along the way, as well as the occasional farm, but now mostly her view was empty road and endless trees. Civilization had dropped off since they turned off I-20 into what Dean called "redneck country." In the backseat, Casey tried to be funny, mimicking the dueling-banjos tune from *Deliverance*, as if "redneck" meant inbreds. Dean was quick to correct Casey that inbreeding hillbillies were in Tennessee and West Virginia, not Texas. But rednecks were territorial and carried shotguns, and they lived by the creed "Don't mess with Texas."

It wasn't the thought of encountering inbred hillbillies or gun-toting rednecks that had Sarah spooked. It was the legions of spiky pines, spruce and cedars pressing so close to the road. These weren't the benign oak and pecan trees that stood in small clusters around White Rock Lake where she walked her dog on weekends. Out here, the trees crowded together, their branches intertwined in a constant battle for space. Choking out the gaps between the trees, thickets of brush and briars left no room for a hiking trail.

Sarah's father, the incurable nature lover, had taught her about things to watch out for in the wilds. Even from the moving vehicle, Sarah could spot the copses of stinging nettles and poison ivy that infested the overgrown forest. If only she had inherited her father's love of exploring the untamed wilderness she might have been thrilled about where Dean and his friends were taking her.

Dean offered Sarah the thermos. "Hot coffee?"

She shook her head. "No thanks."

"Not a morning person, are you?" he observed.

After three lust-filled months of dating, she was afraid he was beginning to see her flaws. Nothing like their first road trip together to bring them out. Sarah didn't care. She was putting her life in this man's hands. "Are you sure we aren't lost?"

Dean looked offended. "I know how to follow a map." Okay, not the type to stop and ask for directions.

"I'm not saying you don't, sweetie." She touched his leg to let him know she wasn't challenging his masculinity. "It's just…every road looks the same." In the city, Sarah always had her bearings, but out here in the sticks she couldn't tell east from west.

"We're right on course." He patted her leg. "Just relax and enjoy the ride."

"Sorry, I'm being a worry wart." Sarah felt like a child now. "I've never done anything like this before."

Dean gave her the confident smile that always melted her. "Trust me. It will be fun."

The thrill of adventure, Sarah mused. That was what had initially attracted her to Mr. Rugged Outdoors, whom she'd met while kayaking with her girlfriends. After ending a dull ten-year marriage to never-gets-his-butt-off-the-couch Barry, Sarah had craved adventure. And she found that in spades with Dean Stratton. In three glorious months, he had already taken her rock climbing, hiking, dancing, rollerblading, and they had run a 5K race together to raise money for a children's hospital. Dean was big into volunteering for Dallas charities, which scored him double bonus points. Sarah often wondered if this man was too good to be true.

They weren't a full-on couple yet. Neither brought up the R-word, but they were more than just casual lovers. She was dating Dean exclusively; hopefully he didn't have another woman or two on the side. She couldn't know for sure, but at least they spent every weekend together. That was a good sign, right?

If she allowed herself, Sarah could easily fall for Dean, but the scars from a bitter divorce were still fresh. She knew the perils of moving too fast and tapped the brakes every time she came close to losing self-control. For now, she focused on living in the moment.

"Where *are* we going exactly?" It was Meg who asked the question. The pixie-cute blonde sat in the backseat with her newlywed husband, Casey, their fingers intertwined.

"It's a surprise," Dean said to his friends from California.

"It's a haunted house, isn't it?" Casey said.

"Could be." Dean winked at Sarah.

Meg raised her coffee cup. "Here's to another wild Ghost Squad exploration."

"Hell yeah to that," said Casey, tapping his wife's cup with his bottle of Mountain Dew. "High adventure, here we come!"

Sarah looked out her side window and held her breath.

Two nights ago, Sarah had nearly choked on her dinner when she learned what Dean, Casey and Meg liked to do for kicks. They were Urban Explorers, meaning they snuck into rundown, abandoned buildings as a hobby. They actually belonged to an underground organization that mapped out sites you could explore in different cities—boarded-up warehouses, condemned churches and office buildings, usually in sections of the city that had gone to the grave.

Urban exploring was illegal, and Sarah couldn't believe she was dating a man who sometimes broke the law. "We're just trespassing," Dean had said like it was no big deal. "The buildings are completely vacant. We explore for a few hours, shoot some video, take a few photos and then go home. No harm done."

"We don't leave any trash behind," Meg added, as if that was a selling point.

"We always leave the place the way we found it," Casey piped in, finishing her thought. He finished a lot of Meg's thoughts—and her beers, and the leftover food on her plate. The guy had an insatiable appetite. In contrast, Meg barely nibbled the lettuce off her burger.

Despite their little hang-ups, Sarah liked Dean's friends. They treated her with kindness and had accepted her into the fold.

The three had given themselves a nickname—the Ghost Squad. It wasn't enough to comb through empty buildings. That was kid's stuff. Dean, Casey and Meg searched for abandoned dwellings claimed to be haunted.

Sarah was afraid of the dark, heights, tight spaces—and, as general rule, always played it safe. Over several rounds of beers, the three of them had seduced Sarah into believing urban exploring was the most-fun thing to do on earth.

When they had Sarah good and tipsy, Dean sprang the news that he had found the perfect building to explore this weekend. It wasn't in Dallas, but three hours away in the East Texas woods. Casey and Meg had flown here from LA, specifically for this UE adventure, even though Dean wasn't divulging the details. The three had begged Sarah to join them until she finally caved.

Now, as Sarah watched the pines roll by and imagined what exploring an old house would be like, she wondered if she could handle the Ghost Squad's idea of adventure. She had almost backed out this morning but knew how much this trip meant to Dean.

He put his hand on her leg, reassuring her. Sarah put her hand on his and forced herself to smile. Needing to distract her mind from her nervousness, she looked back at Meg and Casey. All Sarah knew about the couple was that Casey managed a surfboard shop in Venice Beach and Meg worked as a nurse in the cancer ward at a children's hospital.

"So how long have you two been married?" Sarah asked.

Meg beamed and squeezed Casey's hand. "Six fabulous months."

Sarah, still feeling the pain from her own failed marriage, wondered if Meg would still be this in love ten years from now. Sarah hoped finding true love was not just a myth.

Casey grinned. "We had a totally kick-ass wedding and honeymoon down in Cabo. Dean was there. Remember that, buddy?"

"How could I forget?"

"Let me warn you, Sarah," Meg said. "You're boyfriend can be a lunatic."

"Yeah," said Casey. "The way we got married was *his* crazy idea."

Meg dug into her backpack. "I've got the wedding video on my iPad."

"Guys, don't pull that thing out," Dean said, a look of worry on his face.

"I'd like to see it," Sarah insisted. "I need to know what I'm getting into."

"I still can't believe we did this." Meg handed her the iPad and pressed Play on the screen. The video started as a slow-motion montage edited to the song "Marry Me" by Train. Meg was putting on a wedding dress, along with a parachute pack and helmet. Casey and Dean, wearing tuxedos and parachute gear, did shots of tequila at an airfield next to a plane. Another woman, a pretty redhead with a too-perfect body in a bridesmaid's dress, was hanging all over Dean.

Sarah couldn't help feel the burn of jealousy.

The video cut to the plane being airborne. Beside an open door that looked out to blue sky, a Mexican minister stood with the two couples as Meg and Casey said their vows. The music changed to grunge rock and they all jumped out of the plane. As they fell at mach speed, the two couples came together in midair and held hands, cheering at the top of their lungs. The rest of the video was filled with fast cuts of surfing, nights of drinking, salsa dancing and drunk kissing. At the sight of Dean lip-locking with the redhead, Sarah handed the iPad back to Meg. "Wow, looks like you guys had a wild time."

Dean looked at Sarah apologetically. "That's why I didn't want you to see it."

"It's no big deal." She looked back out the window at the passing trees.

2

The Range Rover pulled into the gravel lot of a rustic gas station and roadhouse called the Lazy Armadillo. All the deer skulls that covered the outer walls didn't put Sarah any more at ease. Neither did the mural of the Confederate flag. Now that they'd finally found an oasis within the pines, the idea of encountering backwoods rednecks rose a level on her fear meter.

Dean swiveled in his seat. "Okay, gang, last pit stop before the expedition begins."

"Me first." Meg hopped out and dashed to the restroom.

"She's got a tiny bladder," Casey said, shaking his head. Then, picking up some kind of unspoken guy signal from Dean, Casey climbed out too. "Come to think of it, I could drain the lizard myself."

Sarah watched the surfer dude head into the gas station and then looked back at Dean.

He gave her a mischievous grin. "Alone at last. Come here."

They both leaned forward and their lips magnetically found one another. She loved this stage—all the kissing, the tingles, the butterflies in the stomach. Wished it could always be like this, but eventually men took more interest in sports, or their careers, or drinking with their buddies. Or, in her ex-husband Barry's case, just quit trying, or even caring.

Dean's not like that, argued the inner voice that still believed in happily ever after. *He's the complete package.* She considered herself lucky to find a man who was good looking, stayed fit, had a stable career as an architect, and a sense of humor to boot. He was also a gentleman, with more than one romantic bone in his body. During their first month of dating, she had mentally checked off every box on her ideal-man checklist. The last test had been in the bedroom. After years of watching Barry clip his toenails in bed and the predictable goodnight pecks on the lips before rolling over and going to sleep, Sarah demanded the universe send her a man who knew how to make love to her.

Sarah and Dean had waited four long, torturous weeks. When the big moment finally came, he had deftly found every zone of her body that shot off fireworks. She liked him so much now that her biggest fear was not being enough for him.

Dean pulled back from their kissing. "You've been so quiet this morning. You're not having second thoughts, are you?"

"No, but I'd be lying if I said I was comfortable with sneaking into an old house."

"It's good to break out of your comfort zone."

"I've never done anything illegal before."

"My good little Catholic girl." He went in for a second kiss.

Sarah leaned back. "We could get arrested."

Dean sighed. "We always take great measures not to get caught. But even if that happened, it's just a misdemeanor. I'd pay your fine, of course."

"My chivalrous lawbreaker." Sarah had to admit the element of danger made this exciting. "Have you ever gone to jail?"

"No. We always choose buildings where there aren't any people around. There are some risks, but for the most part it's safe."

"What do you get out of doing this?" she asked.

Dean looked out the windshield. "When I was a kid, my friends and I used to go exploring in the woods near our neighborhood. We found an old house back there that had been abandoned. All the windows were broken and the front door stood open. We had so much fun searching all the rooms, finding treasures left behind, weathered books and furniture. I still have a jar of antique marbles that I found hidden under the stairs of that house." He reached over and stroked her hair. "Each time I explore old buildings, I get to feel like a kid again."

"Sounds nice."

Dean was so sure of himself that it was easy to trust him. Sarah closed her eyes as his fingers caressed her temple. Her peaceful moment was broken when a truck on giant tires crunched the gravel beside them. An older guy with silver hair and thick sideburns sat behind the wheel. He leered down at Sarah and spat tobacco chaw into a cup.

"There he is!" Dean hopped out and walked toward the truck. "How's it going, man?"

The lean, muscular truck driver hopped down and

shook Dean's hand. "Good to see you again, my friend."

Sarah raised an eyebrow. Dean hadn't mentioned meeting up with anybody. She got out and approached the two men, who couldn't have come from more different backgrounds. Dean was dressed in brand-new hiking clothes, while his buddy wore dusty jeans and a Southern Comfort T-shirt with the sleeves cut off, exposing tattooed biceps. They laughed and carried on like old friends.

Dean said, "Sarah, come over here and meet my buddy Ronnie."

Ronnie tipped his grease-stained ball cap. "How do you do, ma'am?"

Sarah summoned a polite smile. "Nice to meet you."

He continued to gleam. "We don't see many pretty women out here. Guess I need to come visit the city to find me a lady." He elbowed Dean. "You always bring the pretty ones."

At Ronnie's words, Sarah looked at Dean. *How many other women has he brought out here?*

* * *

Inside the general store Casey was perusing candy bars, trying to decide between a King Size Snickers or a PayDay, when Meg suddenly hugged his waist. "Don't look now, but the creep at the register's staring us down."

Casey glanced over his shoulder. The thick-bearded guy sitting behind the counter chewing a piece of beef jerky looked right out of the cast of *Swamp People*. Casey put a protective arm around his wife. "He's just envious that I'm married to the hottest girl on the planet."

"Ahhh." She blushed.

"Who wouldn't want to stare at your ass?" He squeezed her butt and nodded his headed at the redneck.

Meg punched Casey's arm. "Don't egg him on."

Casey laughed. He loved teasing his wife.

Shaking her head, she pulled him by the hand. "Let's find a gift for Jessie. I promised to bring her back a souvenir from Texas."

The nine-year-old girl was one of Meg's patients going through cancer treatments. Jessie had already lost all of her hair and was not expected to survive past the summer. Meg, who entertained her patients with hand-puppet shows, believed she could help children heal through giving them love and attention. Casey hoped she was right, but feared getting too close to patients like Jessie was eventually going to crush Meg's spirit.

The creep at the register kept watching them as they entered a section of the store cluttered with crappy souvenirs that can only be found at a Texas truck stop. One shelf was full of dead animals that had been resurrected by a taxidermist with a twisted sense of humor.

Casey picked up a stuffed armadillo with a shellacked toad riding on its saddle. "I bet Jessie would love one of these."

"Hardy-har-har."

"OK, how about the petrified cow patty?"

Meg gave him the look she gave her two nephews when they acted up. "Will you be serious for five minutes?"

"Fine."

While she checked out a shelf of snow globes with scorpions in them, Casey stopped at a rack of trucker's hats.

Outside the window, he noticed Dean and Sarah talking to one of the local rednecks. Sarah, looking bored, noticed Casey and waved.

He waved back and then looked at Meg. "What do you think of Sarah?"

"I like her. Why?"

Casey shrugged. "She's different from the women Dean usually dates."

Meg snorted. "Yeah, she's got a brain."

"I'm not sure she's Ghost Squad material. She seems so delicate. Remember that rock-climbing instructor, Marley? Now *she* was a match for Dean."

"Marley was fun around you guys, but she was a total bitch to me in private." Meg looked out the window. "Sarah's sweet and genuine. Give her a chance." She picked up a teddy bear wearing a cowboy hat. "I think Jessie would like this."

Casey nodded. "Hey, what do you think about me getting a hat?" He put on a trucker's hat that read I SHAVED MY BALLS FOR THIS?

Meg shook her head and went to the register.

* * *

Sarah didn't know what to make of Ronnie. One moment he was being polite to her, answering "yes, ma'am" and "no, ma'am", then the next he was stripping Sarah out of her clothes with his eyes. Dean was too busy looking over a map on the hood of his car to notice.

When Meg and Casey came back outside, Dean did a round of introductions. "Ronnie runs the East Texas

Chapter for Urban Explorers."

Ronnie kicked a pebble with his boot. "Well, the chapter's down to a member of one now. Folks out here could give a rat's ass about exploring places. They'd rather be drinking at the Armadillo."

Casey snapped his fingers. "Hey, I remember you. We've exchanged emails. You submitted some wicked asylum photos for our website."

"Are we going to the asylum?" Meg asked with so much glee Sarah wondered if the girl needed to be checked in.

"No," Dean answered. "Where we're going's even better. And Ronnie's our guide."

"Are you going to finally tell us?" Casey whined.

"Not yet."

"At least tell us if the building's haunted," Meg said.

"Oh, it's haunted all right," said Ronnie.

Meg clapped her hands and hopped up and down.

Sarah's stomach clenched. She suddenly had the urge to pee. "I'll be right back." She hurried into the gas station and walked past a smoking cashier who followed her with his eyes. She locked herself in the filthy ladies' room. Her heart was a panicky little bird flying around in its cage. She squatted over the grimy toilet without touching it and relieved herself. After pulling up her panties and cargo shorts, she looked at herself in the mirror, willing the fluttering canary in her chest to settle. "You can do this."

Someone knocked at the door. "Hey, Sarah, everything all right?" Meg's voice called.

Sarah wiped her eyes and then let her in. Meg offered a sisterly look. "You okay, hon?"

She nodded.

Meg caressed her arm. "My first time was scary too. A two-story abandoned warehouse in South LA. I kept worrying I was going to fall through the floor and die."

"Oh that helps." Was this her way of female bonding? Scare the new girl?

Meg shrugged. "Once I got the first building out of the way, it was no big deal. Now it's just a rush."

Sitting on the couch and watching the tube with Barry suddenly sounded appealing. Now she was dating Indiana Jones and running around with a group of adrenaline junkies.

"Don't worry," Meg assured, "there's nothing to fear. Casey, Dean and I have done over a dozen UEs together. We know what we're doing."

Standing at five foot six, Sarah was three inches taller than Meg and had more muscle tone, thanks to yoga and kickboxing classes. If this waif-thin pixie could keep up with the boys, then so could Sarah.

3

At a farm ten miles away, Otis Blevins sat on the dirt floor next to the pigsty, crying and rocking, his head between his knees. His chest wouldn't stop hurting. His beloved Bessie was gone. The house ate her like all his other pigs. Then Otis had come home and found another piglet dead, half-chewed and spit out by its mother. Now he was down to one sow and one piglet. The house would demand them too before long, and then he'd be out of pigs.

The man rocked and sniffled, strings of snot hanging from his nose. "Not fair! Not fair!"

What are you crying about, boy? yelled his grandpa's voice.

Otis looked up and saw Grandpa's ghost standing shin-deep in the pigsty. Dressed in the same bloody clothes that he had shot himself in, his single eye glared from his half-blown-off face.

Otis looked away.

Look at me when I'm talking to you, boy! Blevins men don't cry, you hear me? Now quit your sniveling or I'll get my switch and give you something to cry about.

"Sorry, Grandpa. I ain't crying no more." Otis wiped his runny nose on his sleeve. He didn't want to get a whuppin'.

He wished Mama was here. She'd take him to her special place down in the root cellar where Grandpa couldn't find them.

She isn't coming back, his grandpa's ghost said. *Now get up and finish your chores.*

Otis sucked in his tears and continued filling slops in the trough. Matilda lay in the mud with her little one suckling. Otis hadn't bothered to name the piglet yet. He got too close to his pigs when he gave them names. Last week Matilda birthed a litter of five. Each morning Otis came to feed her, he saw that she had eaten another one. The sow knew what he was up to. She had seen all her pig mates ride off with him in the truck and not come back. Otis knew as surely as blood runs red that Matilda's last piglet had a day or two left before she ate him too.

Once Matilda made her final journey down the well shaft, then what? The house's hunger never quit. It always demanded more, more, more.

As Otis pondered what to do, the house gave him visions of the kind of meat it wanted him to bring next.

4

The white Range Rover that carried the four members of the Ghost Squad followed Ronnie's truck down a narrow dirt road. The constant procession of pine trees marched past their windows. Occasionally, branches raked the sides of the vehicles.

Sarah and Dean hadn't gotten a moment alone to discuss the other girls he had brought out here. She felt a tinge of jealousy and disappointment that she wasn't the first. *So there were other women before you,* her mind argued. *Let it go.*

Her voice of reason was right. She was worrying too much about things he'd done in the past and not allowing herself to enjoy the present. What mattered now was that Dean was including her in something he was passionate about. Sarah stroked his leg, an unspoken truce. He winked and his hand rested on her knee where it belonged.

The vehicles left the road and parked behind a grove of blue spruce. Sarah didn't see any building in sight, just thick trees that towered so high they blocked out the afternoon sun.

Dean killed the engine. "All right, everybody, grab your gear. We're going the rest of the way in Ronnie's truck."

Sarah shivered at the thought of abandoning their car. "Why not drive the whole way?"

Meg explained, "We never park right next to the site…"

"…in case somebody shows up while we're inside," Casey finished.

Dean nodded. "Ronnie works at the owner's pig farm and on weekends comes to this property to clear brush. His truck being at the house won't alarm the owner if he happens by, which he won't, but we're taking precautions anyway."

"How can you be so sure?" Sarah asked.

"Because I know the owner's routine." Ronnie leaned on Sarah's open window, so close she could smell the musk from his armpit. "Otis comes here once every week on Saturday morning. He tinkers with the house and leaves by noon. He won't be back."

This seemed to satisfy Dean and his friends. They transported their backpacks and a cooler to Ronnie's truck and climbed in the flatbed. Ronnie gunned his big engine and drove them back onto the dirt road. The two couples sat with their gear in back, jostling from side to side. Next to Sarah, some dusty chains rattled.

Casey reached into the cooler and pulled out a ham sandwich and a Mountain Dew. He offered to fish out lunch for the rest of the group, but everyone declined. Eating was the last thing on Sarah's mind. Her eyes met Meg's. The glee in the other girl's blue eyes had been replaced by something else. Nervousness? A sense of doom? Meg's leg constantly bounced. The pixie wasn't so fearless after all. While this didn't comfort Sarah, it made her feel closer to

Meg, a sisterhood bonded by dread.

An old country song played in Ronnie's cab. The singer plucked a steel guitar and crooned with a hollow twang.

Leaning against Dean's shoulder, Sarah asked, "How long have you known Ronnie?"

"About a year. We've done two UEs together. He's a good guide."

The truck rounded a curve and drove through an open gate. Everyone gasped in unison as the stone house came into view. With its flat facade covered in ivy, the three-story house reminded Sarah of the small castles she had seen while traveling with her parents across Scotland. Constructed mostly from gray stones, the house could have been built by Druids. The trees grew thick around the house, their branches covering parts of the roof. What stood out most were all the boards covering the windows.

The windows are sealed? Sarah didn't dare voice her concern out loud. She had committed to this expedition and wasn't going to be the one who dragged the group down. She secretly hoped Dean would change his mind about this, but he looked back at everyone and grinned. "Here we are, gang. Let the adventures begin."

"Woo hoo!" Casey cheered and gave poor Meg a hug that tipped her sideways.

They all climbed out and carried their packs and the cooler to the front steps. Engraved on a stone plate above the door was the name BLEVINS. Sarah tilted her head, looking past the ivy walls to the apex of the roof. The building looked massive from this angle.

"This was originally a ranch house back in the 1930s," Dean explained. He took Sarah's hand. "Let's check the lay of the land." They broke away from the group and walked around the exterior.

She noticed strange symbols painted in red on the clapboards. "What are those for?"

"You'll have to ask Ronnie. He knows more about this house than I do." Dean tapped the rock wall with a metal hiking pole.

"What are you doing?" Sarah asked.

"Testing the structure for signs of erosion. We won't go in if I think it's going to cave in on us."

"My super handyman," Sarah said. Dean was an architect by profession; his father was a home builder. They had a business where they bought old houses, refurbished them, and then flipped them for profit. The two of them could talk for hours about drywall and foundation setting.

Sarah felt a certain security in watching Dean work. She followed him around to the backyard, which was overgrown with bunchgrass. All the windows on this side were also boarded up. The back door too. About ten yards from the back of the house, Sarah almost stepped into a large hole.

Dean threw a protective arm across her chest. "Whoa, watch it."

She stopped abruptly, knocking pebbles down a deep shaft. "Shit, that was close."

"Looks like an old well," he said.

There was no barrier around it to give anyone warning. Just even ground and then a dead drop. The shaft was lined with rock walls. A few feet away, a chain hooked to a pulley led down to a rocky floor with shallow water. Sarah thought she made out the skeleton of an animal at the bottom.

"I see you two found the well shaft," Ronnie said from behind them. "I forgot to warn you about that."

Dean said, "You should tell the owner to build a wall around the hole or cover it. Sarah almost fell in."

"Oh man, sorry about that," Ronnie said. "If ya'll are ready, we'll gear up and head inside."

They followed their guide back to the front yard. Casey and Meg had donned matching black-and-yellow caving suits and helmets. Dean put a helmet with a headlamp on Sarah's head and strapped it beneath her chin. He put his hands on her shoulders. "Ready for this?"

She nodded, doing her best to hide her nervousness.

He boosted her courage with a kiss. "You know, Miss Donovan, you're scoring big points by doing this."

"I better be," she teased and pulled him against her for a longer kiss. After they released each other, he geared up with a caving helmet, rock-climbing harness and a pair of fingerless black gloves. Shouldering his backpack, Dean looked damned sexy.

Meg pulled out her camera. "Group photo time!" The two couples posed in front of the house as Ronnie took their picture.

"All right," Ronnie said. "Before we go inside, it's time for a little background."

"Excellent," said Casey. The others agreed.

Ronnie stood on the front steps and patted the thick oak door. "The Old Blevins House is a legend among these parts. No one in Buck Horn will come near here, due to the house's violent history. Are y'all familiar with the Blevins Family Massacre?"

Only Dean nodded. "I read an article about it. It was

fascinating. That's why I brought you guys here."

"So what happened?" Casey asked.

Ronnie said, "From 1968 to 1972, this house and the two hundred acres it sits on was a hippy commune. People were smoking weed, tripping on LSD and fornicating all day and night. It was all free love, sex and drugs until the summer of '72, when something went terribly wrong here. Maybe they took some bad acid, but on one violent night over twenty-five people died in this house. Murders and mass suicides. It was a bloody mess. Some people even vanished without a trace. After that, the house was condemned and has been boarded up ever since." Ronnie lowered his voice. "According to Otis Blevins, who owns this property, the house is full of ghosts."

"Awesome!" Casey walked along the outer wall with a handheld device. "I'm definitely picking up some EMF."

Sarah hugged herself. This was Dean's big surprise? A backwoods house where a bunch of people were murdered? She wished he had told her this last night. She might have been able to back out. She was tempted to just wait outside while the others explored. *No, I came all this way. I'm doing this.* When Dean looked her way with a big grin, Sarah faked a smile.

He threw his arm around her shoulder and kissed her cheek. "This is going to be our best date ever."

Meg snapped photos of the red symbols painted on each window covering. "What are these for?"

"Beats the hell out of me," Ronnie said. "Otis put them there. He ain't right in the head."

"Have you explored inside yet?" Sarah asked.

"No, I've been waiting til I assembled the right group."

As Ronnie went to his truck, Dean took the perch in front of the door to the house. "The building that we're about to enter has been boarded up for over forty years. Front door's the only way in and only way out. No Urban Explorers have been here before us."

"All right, virgin territory!" Casey high-fived Meg.

Dean remained serious. "Our mission is to shoot some quality video and photos for the website and map out the rooms and any pitfalls for future explorers. I want to remind everybody—safety first. Always test the floor before you take a step. And no one wanders off alone. *Capisce*?"

"Rodger Dodger," said Casey.

Sarah and Meg nodded.

Ronnie returned with a pair of bolt cutters. The front door's rusty padlock snapped with one crunch of the cutter's jaws. "I'll replace it with a new one later," he said. The knob was also locked, but after thirty seconds of picking it, Ronnie had the door open.

"Impressive," said Casey.

"I can get into most anything," Ronnie said, winking at Sarah.

She stared at the doorway's gaping maw, and the darkness within stared back. Decades of trapped air wafted out—a mixture of mildew, dust and rotting wood. She swallowed hard.

Dean slipped an arm around her back. "Just stay close to me and you'll be fine."

He and Ronnie entered first, tapping the wood floor with hiking poles.

"The foyer's solid," said Dean and waved the others in.

Sarah switched on her helmet light and the flashlight in

her hand. She followed Casey and Meg into the entryway. The first thing Sarah noticed was a colorful mural painted on the back wall. The paint had faded and was covered in layers of mold and grime, but she could make out peace symbols and hearts and warped landscapes someone had clearly painted while on psychedelic drugs.

Ronnie brought in their cooler and closed the door, sealing off the sunlight. The covered windows provided only thin borders of light. The group spread out. Their beams swished around the darkness, which seemed to stretch to infinity. The sweltering air inside smelled ripe with fungus.

Sarah played her lights along the floor, more mural-painted walls spotted with black mold, the water-stained ceiling. In several places, creepers of ivy had invaded the house. When she looked straight ahead, she realized the others had wandered into another chamber. Their echoing voices sounded like they were walking down a drainage pipe.

"Shit." Already falling behind, Sarah searched the gloom, arms outstretched and feeling her way along the flaking wall. "Dean!?"

"Right here." He appeared from around a corner and touched her hand, causing her to jump.

She squeezed his wrists. "Please don't leave me."

"I won't let you out of my sight." He unraveled a length of rope from his hip and snapped a carabiner onto the front of her harness. "Stay with me the whole time, okay? If you start to get spooked, take some deep breaths."

Tethered to Dean, she followed him into the void.

5

As Sarah fumbled through the darkness behind him, Dean questioned his decision to bring her along. There were too many unknown dangers here, and she had zero experience. Plus, she wasn't much of a climber. The one time he took her rock climbing, she struggled to find the footholds. She never did make it to the top to ring the bell. He had felt disappointed. Sarah had climbed down, visibly upset that he'd pushed her too hard. He was so driven that sometimes he didn't know when to let up.

Now he had to show Sarah how to walk tied to his harness, where to direct her light beams, where not to step. In hindsight, he should have taken her to a building in Dallas first, like the old boarded-up church downtown or the unused elementary school in the slums of West Dallas. Those buildings were perfect for beginners. He had explored them a half-dozen times and knew the terrain well.

As much as Dean loved sharing his favorite hobby with this amazing new woman in his life, Sarah might panic and run off into the darkness. That had happened with his last girlfriend and she fell and broke her nails. Their relationship ended shortly after.

Like it or not, Sarah's safety was in his hands, and he had to make sure he protected her from harm.

He gave her a quick safety lesson on how to move about in an old house. How to test the floor and what pitfalls to watch for. He started to go into all the uses of the rock-climbing gear he'd brought—belay devices, carabiners, cams and quickdraws—and how to tie a knot.

Sarah held up her palms. "Okay, okay, my brain's full. I'll just stick close to you."

Dial it down a bit, Dean, he told himself. He had a bad habit of trying to impress women with his knowledge. A flaw he'd picked up when he was a teenager with bad acne.

Dean kept seven feet of rope between himself and Sarah—short enough to keep his lover close and long enough to give him some slack so he could move in any direction without her bumping into him every few feet. Sarah kept up and began matching him step for step. She was a fast learner and willing to face this challenge with him. He loved that about her. Exploring abandoned buildings together would be a true test of their relationship. Most women he'd dated had failed. He longed to find a woman with whom he could share adventures. He had high hopes that Sarah was going to be the one.

They caught up with the others in a room that appeared to be a den with a hardwood floor. White flashes blinded his eyes as Meg snapped photos, leaving ghost impressions of his friends floating in the air.

"Can you kill the photo-taking for a moment?" Dean switched on his video camera. The spacious den was devoid of furniture. Every room they had explored so far was covered in graffiti. There was no order to the art. It looked as if the hippies had painted the walls whenever they got the whim, often clashing with the themes around them. One mural of dark-winged skeletons had been sketched angrily with black charcoal.

Dean's headlamp beam passed across a rock fireplace and the pocked walls around it. In many places the plaster had fallen, revealing the mortared stones that held the walls in place. More tendrils of ivy bordered the windows and spread across the rocks of the fireplace.

Sarah stepped up beside Dean, placing her hand on his back. "The artwork is pretty out there, isn't it?"

"Yeah, check this out." Dean pointed his flashlight at a mural of naked men and women dancing in a circle around a fire. "Look at this freak." One of the dancers had horns and goat legs.

"That's the goat god, Pan," Sarah said. "He's the god of the trees and all the animals in the forest."

Casey poked his head between them. "And he likes to have orgies with wood nymphs."

Dean sighed, studying the horned beast. "He looks like the devil to me."

Ronnie lit a cigarette and tapped his foot—his way of signaling to keep a move on. The group followed their guide down a hallway through the center of the house. Every few steps, Dean and Ronnie tested the floor with their poles.

They passed a wide staircase that went straight up into the pitch-dark.

Sarah froze and gripped Dean's arm. "Shit, did you guys hear that?"

"What?" asked Dean.

Sarah held her palm against her chest. "I heard the wood creak on the second floor. When I aimed my light upward, I thought I saw a shadow move."

Everyone stood still and listened. Their beams played along the banister, casting striped shadows on the second floor's ceiling.

"You probably heard the house shifting," Ronnie said.

Sarah said, "That doesn't explain the shadow I saw. It looked like someone walked past the railing."

Casey yelled, "Hello, anybody up there?"

Dean hit his arm. "Cut that out. There's nobody in here but us."

Casey held up his EMF device. "Maybe it was a ghost. Shall we go up?"

"Later." Dean walked down the hall. "Let's map out the ground floor first."

Just past the stairway, the hallway opened to a second den with a cement floor. The artwork on the walls was different than the other rooms—orderly, with white circles painted on every brick. Inside the circles were pagan symbols and pentagrams. On the floor, melted candles orbited a large circle that must have been ten feet in circumference. In the center, Dean recognized the stick-figure marking that had been painted on the clapboards outside. He shot some video, getting glimpses of animal skulls as all the lights passed over them.

Sarah knelt beside Dean. "What is all this?"

"Strange, isn't it?"

"They were sacrificing something here." Casey's flashlight spotlighted a wooden bowl full of bones.

"Ewww." Meg hovered behind her husband.

Dean relished the shocked expressions on his friends' faces. "Ronnie, tell them about the Blevins witches."

Their guide stepped into the circle. "The hippies who lived on this commune were actually a coven of witches and warlocks. They practiced Wicca." Ronnie spun around with his flashlight, lighting up all the pagan symbols. "This was their ceremonial room."

* * *

Sarah stared at the bowl of bones. "This couldn't have been done by Wiccans."

Dean did a double take. "How would you know?"

"Because my grandmother's a Wiccan. She told me witches don't slaughter animals."

Ronnie looked at Sarah with a devious twinkle in his eyes. "Well, the Blevins witches practiced black magic. The coven was ruled by a high priestess, Lenora Ravenmoon Blevins. She was Otis's mother. He was only six the night the massacre happened."

The thought that people had died in this house made Sarah shudder.

Ronnie paused to light another cigarette.

"And…" said Casey, "…what happened to them all?"

Ronnie said, "The night of the massacre, one of the coven members, Abigail Blackwood, managed to escape through the woods. She wandered into the Lazy Armadillo with blood covering her body. She was hysterical, muttering that all her family members were dead."

Dean said, "The police searched the house. They found several of the witches slaughtered throughout, downstairs and upstairs, as if someone had gone on a killing spree."

"Did Abigail say who killed her coven?" Meg asked.

"Police never got the chance to ask her," answered Ronnie. "While the sheriff and his men were out searching, she killed two of the deputies and snuck back into the house. You know those stairs we passed? That's where Abigail hung herself from the second-floor railing." Ronnie paused for dramatic effect. "Over twenty-five people died that night, including some children."

Meg gasped. "Not the children too."

"There was one survivor," Ronnie said. "The police found Otis down in the cellar. They also found the decapitated heads of the witches mounted on sticks, but never found their bodies. Police dug for a mass grave but turned up nothing." Ronnie smiled as if he was enjoying scaring them. "The mystery remains unsolved."

"I call bullshit," Sarah said. "You made this story up to scare us." Sarah was no fool. She had toured haunted houses and seen carnival sideshows. The creepy back story was all a part of the grand illusion. Ronnie must have broken in here and set up this ceremonial room. The bowl of bones was a nice touch. Had Dean helped him? Did her boyfriend get some kind of sick thrill out of scaring people?

She elbowed Dean's arm. "You knew about this, didn't you?"

He chuckled, "Yeah, I thought it would be more fun if I kept the house's history a surprise."

"I don't like surprises," Sarah said.

"This is not a hoax," Dean defended. "Some witches really lived and died here." He shone his light across the chalked graffiti on the walls. "What you see is what they left behind."

Meg hovered next to Sarah. "What if whoever killed the witches comes back while we're here?"

"Relax," said Dean. "This happened decades ago."

"So you two aren't just putting us on?" Sarah said.

"See all these dark stains on the floor and walls," Ronnie shone his light on a black splotch on the floor. "This is where half of the people were slaughtered."

"Enough, guys," Meg said. "You've succeeded in spooking us. Can we leave this room now?"

"I second that." Sarah gave Dean a nudge.

The group explored the rest of the ground floor, finding a dining room with peeling wallpaper, a grimy kitchen that had been overtaken by mold and spiders, and a walk-in pantry stocked with swollen canned goods that looked ready to burst.

Casey picked up a can leaking black goo. "Spinach, anybody?" When no one laughed, he set the can down. "Tough crowd." He opened a door at the back of the pantry. "Hey, I found the cellar."

Sarah looked over his shoulder. A stone stairway led down to a black abyss. She backed away, shaking her head. "No way am I going down there." She looked at Dean. "Sorry, but the cellar's where I draw the line. If you guys want to go down there, have at it. I'll wait outside."

Dean nodded. "Casey, let's save this for last. I'd like to see what's upstairs."

The group returned to the center of the house. Sarah waited patiently with Meg and Casey as Dean and Ronnie tested the strength of each wooden stair ascending to the second floor. The staircase groaned a little but was surprisingly sturdy.

When Sarah joined Dean at the top, he rehooked his rope onto her harness. She tugged at him. "You must love having your woman on a leash."

"It's good for my ego."

She laughed. "As if your head could get any bigger…"

Dean grinned and stroked her arm. "Are you game for some more thrills?"

"That depends…do you have any more stories about ghosts and dead witches?"

"No, history lesson's over. The rest of the tour is just exploring dusty old rooms."

"Good. I don't think my heart could handle any more."

"Can it handle this?" Dean pulled her into his arms and kissed her.

The touch of his lips spread warmth through her body. Sarah smiled and released her breath. "Now that is the kind of surprise I like."

"Having you here means a lot to me." He was being serious.

They kissed again. It seemed different than all the other times, softer, with more feeling, as if they'd crossed into new-relationship territory. She had promised herself she would take things slow and here she was, enchanted by this man. The spell broke when she noticed Ronnie watching them from the shadows. His headlamp was off and all she could see was a firefly of glowing ash from his cigarette.

"Soon as you lovebirds are ready, we'll keep going."

"We're right behind you," said Dean.

Sarah walked within the safety of the middle of the

pack, as the five explored single-file down the second-floor hallway. They probed empty bedrooms with their lights. Noises creaked throughout the house, as if protesting the disturbance they were making.

When they reached a second stairway at the end of the hall, Casey and Ronnie got into an argument about where to go next. Their guide wanted to keep pushing upward, while Casey and Meg preferred to explore the second floor further.

"It's nothing but empty rooms," Ronnie said. "The top floor's the attic. That's what I been wantin' to see."

"Go right ahead," said Casey. "We'll stay down here."

"Suit yourself." Ronnie started up the narrow staircase, tapping each step angrily with his pole.

The two couples gathered at the foot of the stairs. Dean whispered, "I thought the plan was to stick together."

"He's moving us too fast," Casey complained.

"Yeah," Meg said. "I barely get a chance to take pictures."

"You guys don't have to babysit us," Casey said. "We've done plenty of these, just the two of us."

"Sarah, what about you?" Dean asked. "Want to explore the attic?"

"Only if you want to."

"I need to shoot some video and photos of the attic for the website. How about you and I check it out and then we'll all meet down here in a half hour?"

"Sounds good to me, man." Casey bumped fists with Dean.

Sarah followed her boyfriend up the creaking steps. Unlike the first stairway, which was wide, with curving banisters, this staircase was steep and extremely narrow. The cedar walls rubbed against her shoulders as she climbed. With every step the passage groaned like the hull of an old wooden ship. At the midpoint, the stairway turned a sharp corner.

Sarah was nearly out of breath by the time they reached the top floor. Their lights probed a vaulted ceiling draped with cobwebs. A broad attic with rock walls stretched the length of the house. At the far end, light leaked in through a partially covered window. There was a hole in one corner where birds fluttered through to their roost.

Sarah walked with Dean to the center. They took their time as he tested each floorboard.

"The floor's sturdy," Ronnie called from ahead of them. "No need to tap the boards." He stood in an island of darkness. An odd array of shapes took form around him. When their lights shone across what Ronnie had found, Sarah gasped.

6

On the second floor, Casey felt pulled in a hundred directions. So many places to explore. Rooms and corridors, closets and crawl spaces that hadn't been encountered by a human in decades. He felt the thrill of an archaeologist who had discovered an unexplored tomb, searching for lost treasure. The adrenaline pumping through his chest was the same way he felt sitting on his surfboard in Malibu, waiting for the perfect swell.

Every direction offered unlimited possibilities. But he was tethered to Meg and she had her own mind about where to explore. Too many times they walked in opposite directions and were halted by the tug of the other. Casey usually gave in, because Meg was his girl and he liked to please her—to a fault sometimes. He loved to hear her squeal with excitement, like she did when she was riding cowgirl on top of him. But today he didn't want to be dragged around by her leash.

He stepped into the hallway to search another room, but Meg had anchored her legs to the floor. The rope snagged against the threshold. "Come on," he tugged. Oddly, he couldn't budge her. "Meg, let's check this next room."

She didn't answer.

Sighing, Casey walked back and saw that she was standing with her back to him.

He tugged the rope again. "Are you coming or what?"

Meg remained statue-still, facing the mottled wall. Casey shone his light over her shoulder. The wall, speckled in black mold, had a faded mural of a woman wrapped in vines. Her eyes were large black chasms.

"Hellooo?" He waved his hand in front of Meg's catatonic eyes. When she didn't so much as blink, he shook her shoulder and she snapped out of her trance.

"Hey..." she griped in protest, "...why are you shaking me?"

"You were totally tranced out." He examined her pupils. "You didn't pop any X, did you?"

"Of course not."

"Promise?"

"Casey, I never do X without you."

"Well, answer me next time. You were freaking me out."

"Sorry. Guess I spaced."

"Probably because you skipped lunch. Want me to get you a sandwich?"

"I'm not hungry."

"Well, snack on a PowerBar or something." He fished into his backpack and gave her one of his. "Let's untie ourselves for a while."

"You sure?"

"The floor feels pretty stable. See?" He danced an Irish jig on the floorboards, making her laugh.

"Okay, but stay close, Lord of the Dance." She pinched his nipple.

"You too, Squeaky." He swatted her behind.

Meg giggled. She suddenly got aroused. He could tell because her breasts swelled through her spandex shirt, her nipples hardening. A naughty look in her eyes, she walked up to Casey and cupped his crotch. "How about a quickie?"

Meg was big into having sex in strange places. They'd done it in nearly every abandoned building they had explored together. It had become a tradition.

"I'm totally game, but later. I want to keep exploring."

She pouted. "I may not be horny later."

"Oh yes you will." He pulled her against his chest and squeezed her ass. "We'll sneak off for some fun in a while, okay?"

"Okay."

Casey unhooked the rope and set Meg free to roam. The room flashed, as she took pictures of the strange mural of the goddess.

Casey hurried down the hall to a room near the end. The others had passed by it without poking their lights into it. But he had glimpsed something. He stepped into the room and the first thing he noticed was the smell—fresh Pine-Sol. While the other rooms were caked in decades of dust and fungus, this room had been recently swept, the floorboards polished. Someone had been in the house before them and taken extra care of this room. It was a feminine boudoir, with lavender wallpaper that had been wiped with disinfectant, the tears mended, albeit poorly. Several spots looked as if someone had dragged a rake down the wall. Floral curtains that had seen better years hung at the windows. They were open, offering a spectacular view of the back side of the clapboards.

Casey approached the object he had seen earlier—an antique vanity with a chair and oval mirror. The light from his headlamp reflected in the badly scratched glass. Perched on the table was a wooden picture frame. A photo of a woman stared back at him, her eyes haunting. She was no beauty queen. Her dark hair was long and wavy, parted in a 1970s hairstyle. The vanity's whole display looked vintage, except for the unlit candles that circled the frame. They still had Walmart stickers on them.

Casey rummaged through the vanity's many drawers. They were full of makeup, spools of thread, countless buttons and jewelry. *Cha-ching! Cha-ching!*

He glanced over his shoulder to see if anyone was looking and then stuffed all the rings and necklaces into his backpack. As soon as he zipped up his booty, his conscience nagged him, reminding him that this house still belonged to somebody. Mr. Pine-Sol Cleaner would probably be upset if he discovered the jewelry missing. Sighing, Casey put the jewelry back. He was a treasure hunter, but not a thief.

He continued digging through the vanity. In a bottom drawer he found jars full of hair and what looked to be fingernail clippings, and were those teeth? *Sick.* He put the jars back. Another drawer contained several human-shaped figures made from burlap. They had buttons for eyes. He picked one up. It was filled with some kind of herbs that smelled rank.

In the reflection of the mirror, someone passed by the doorway. Must have been Meg, off on her own scavenger hunt.

Casey called to her, "Hey, come see this."

She didn't respond.

He stepped back into the second-floor hallway. "Meg!" Still no response. She was probably in one of the far rooms. He didn't see any light from her headlamp. He waited for her camera to flash again. Several seconds passed. The passage remained dark.

He poked his flashlight beam into each room he passed. A few had closed closet doors. He wondered what other interesting things he could find. He felt so tempted to continue exploring on his own.

But first he had to make sure his wife was all right.

Casey cupped his hands and called her name again. It was not like Meg to stray off by herself. Whenever they did urban exploring without being roped together, they always kept within twenty feet of one another. It was one thing to venture farther down the hall, but if she left the floor to explore another level, he was going to be royally pissed. His light illuminated a banister that overlooked the ground floor. "Meg, where are you?" Only his voice echoed back.

When he reached the stairway leading down, he found her hiking shoe sitting on the top step. Casey picked it up and swiveled his headlamp beam across the second-floor landing. The dark hallway stretched in two directions, empty. Looking down, he spotted her second shoe at the bottom of the stairs. He walked down and scooped it up. "Meg, what kind of game are you playing?"

Again, no response.

Exploring the ground floor, he came upon her socks and belt in the hallway, laid out like a trail of bread crumbs.

Part Two

The Blevins Witches

7

"Oh, wow," Sarah said, putting her hand on Dean's shoulder.

The center of the attic was cluttered with furniture and boxes covered in plastic. Ronnie was in the midst of it, rummaging through a crate. "Lordy, Lordy, look at all this stuff that's just been left here to gather dust."

"We can't take any of it, of course," Dean reminded his friend. "All this belongs to the owner of the house."

"Shit, Otis probably hasn't been up here in twenty years."

"But still…"

Ronnie tossed a claw hammer back in a box.

"There's no harm in looking, is there?" Sarah asked.

Dean answered, "As long as we leave things the way we found them."

Sarah loved antiques. She opened the doors of an armoire and was embraced by a waft of dust. Several moth-eaten dresses hung on a rod. They looked absolutely vintage. Standing beside the wardrobe was a Singer sewing machine and a headless cloth mannequin with pushpins all over it.

"Check this out." Dean showed her a viewfinder with

double-printed photos in the picture holder. He placed the metal-and-glass goggles over Sarah's eyes. Black-and-white photos popped out in 3D. Nude men and women having sex in an array of positions. She laughed at the depictions of old-timey pornography.

Dean winked. "We should try some of these."

Sarah blushed and flipped the viewfinder over. "It's an Underwood and Underwood, circa 1901."

"You know about antiques?" he asked.

"I go antiquing with my mom and grandmother whenever they come to visit. It's a Donovan tradition."

"Most of this stuff belonged to Lenora Blevins," Ronnie said. "Her parents gave her this house."

"Were they witches too?" Dean asked.

"The Blevins coven goes back hundreds of years."

Sarah got on her knees and opened a trunk on the floor. It was full of books on witchcraft and black magic. She flipped through one of them. It contained lots of spells and illustrations of demons. One chapter was called "How to Summon Evil Spirits." This definitely wasn't typical Wiccan magic. Sarah's grandmother would never own a book like this. Sarah got the heebie-jeebies just looking at all the demonic images and put it aside.

Beneath the spell books she found a framed photo of a woman with long brown hair. Beside her stood a boy with buckteeth and bad posture. He was wearing overalls and holding a baby pig.

"That's Otis when he was a boy," Ronnie said. "He was born a retard." He leaned over Sarah's shoulder and tapped the photo. "And that there's his mother, Lenora."

"The coven's high priestess," Sarah mused.

Dean said, "She was the only person the police never found. They found her bloody clothes in the cellar but no body. And her head wasn't among the trophies."

"That's right," Ronnie said. "Folks back in Buck Horn think it was Lenora who did all the killings. Ask any of the elders in town and they'll tell you she was completely batty. If you so much as looked at Lenora wrong, she'd give you the evil eye."

The woman's wild eyes in the photo made Sarah feel uneasy. She set it aside and rummaged through the trunk. At the bottom, she found a large scrapbook. The first few pages were crude children's drawings of the house, a collection of feathers, the crumbling remains of what might have been a dried flower. She flipped the page and found a display of Polaroid photos.

"Dean, come look at this."

He kneeled beside her. "More naked photos?"

"No, it's the Blevins coven."

A group photo taken in front of the rock house showed Lenora Ravenmoon Blevins sitting in front of a crowd of twenty-plus people. Most were young women, with only five men among the coven. Everyone wore the long hair styles and colorful clothes—bell-bottom jeans, striped pants, halter tops and jumpsuits—that were so common in the early '70s. Sarah counted five kids, most of them toddlers and infants. Otis, again posing with his pig, looked to be the oldest of the children.

On another page were individual photos with captions beneath them. "Looks like somebody kept a record of those who died." Sarah read the names out loud. "Jimmy Murray, murdered in the front den. Mona Jennings, stabbed to death in the kitchen. Emma Blevins, Connie Blackwood, and five other women were murdered in the ceremonial room." She turned the page. "Esther Cummings, found dead in her closet. Lizzy Blevins drowned four children in the bathtub, then drowned herself. Dragomir Stewart hung himself in the attic." Sarah counted off more names then looked at Ronnie. "Six people hung themselves in the attic?"

Ronnie said, "Pretty fucked up, ain't it?"

"But why?"

"Who knows? People do crazy shit when they're on acid."

Dean said, "The article I read said that the six people had locked themselves in the attic. The door was still locked when the police got there. They found three of the men and three of the women hanging from the rafters."

Sarah began to grow concerned. She wasn't superstitious, but being in the house where so many people had died so violently made her shiver.

The last photo was a newspaper clipping of Abigail Blackwood. According to Ronnie and Dean, she had been one of the cult members who had escaped but then returned to the house and hung herself from the second-floor banister.

"Why would Abigail come back here and hang herself?"

Dean said, "Police never figured out why. They decided that maybe she helped with the killings and came back to join her coven in death. Definitely bizarre."

Sarah put the scrapbook away and closed the trunk, as if locking it away could protect her from the Blevins family curse. "I think we should leave right now."

"What for?"

"What if this house is cursed?"

Dean snorted. "Seriously?" He rubbed her leg. "Sarah, you're getting spooked over something that happened four decades ago."

"No, there's a bad pattern in this house. Everyone who's come in here has died."

"Otis is still alive," he countered.

"But he lost his family here. Maybe that's why he boarded up the windows. To keep people out. We shouldn't be in here."

Dean sighed. "We can't go yet, I still need to explore the cellar and shoot some video."

Sarah touched his hand. "Please don't. Earlier, I got a bad feeling about the cellar. Worse than any part of the house."

"Ronnie, tell her there's nothing to worry about." Dean stood and looked around. "Ronnie?"

Sarah heard the attic door shut. "Why's he leaving us?" She suddenly wanted to be anywhere but in this attic. Her heart beating with panic, she hurried to the door and turned the knob but the door protested and refused to open. Ronnie had locked it from the other side.

8

Ten miles away, Otis Blevins sat in the gloom of his living room, drinking whiskey from a bottle. His eyes welled up with tears. He missed being a part of a big family. Most of all, he missed being with Mama, back when she could still hold him in her arms.

As he stared at the wall, he reflected back to those dark, final days, when he was six years old and the coven was falling apart…

June 1972

Little Otis walked barefoot through the first floor of the commune's house. Running ahead of him was his baby pig Jasper. The house smelled of incense and burning grass. The place was so crowded, people occupied all the rooms. In one den, they slept on the floor in sleeping bags at all hours of the day. In the kitchen, women were often chatting and adding new smells to the house with their cooking. There was always music playing in the community room. Everybody smoked, passing joints and bongs to one another, eating mushrooms, laughing one minute, crying the next. Dragomir played guitar and some of the others beat on drums.

On good nights, Otis's family sang and danced around a fire in the backyard, some of them naked.

But tonight wasn't a good night. The grown-ups were fighting again. He could hear them yelling down the hall. Otis covered his ears as he and Jasper entered the ceremonial room.

Mama was at the center of the circle, yelling at the others. "This is *my* coven. *I* am the high priestess. Not you or you or you. And definitely not Abigail."

"You've lost your way, Lenora," Sister Abigail challenged. She was wearing Mama's sacred cloak. "It's time someone else led the coven. And they've chosen me."

"No. Never!" Mama yelled and pointed to Abigail. "I want you out of my house! All of you, just get the fuck out!"

"This house belongs to the coven now," Dragomir said. "You put all our names on the deed, remember?"

Mama walked the circle, getting in people's faces. "I gave y'all a place to live, taught you all my magic, and now you turn against me?"

"It is *you* who have turned against *us*," Abigail said. "The woman we followed is gone. And now you have a demon inside you, Lenora." The girl began chanting, "Demon be gone! Demon be gone!"

The other grown-ups joined in the chanting. "Demon be gone! Demon be gone!"

Mama screamed and attacked Abigail, clawing her face.

The men grabbed Mama's arms and pulled her away.

Abigail wiped blood off her cheeks and pointed. "Put her in the Pit of Darkness."

"No!" Lenora cried.

"Mama!" Otis tried to help her, but someone picked him up. He cried, reaching for her, as the men and women dragged Mama, kicking and screaming, down into the cellar.

9

"Meg, where the hell are you?" Casey yelled on the bottom floor. The trail of her clothing led to the open cellar door. He picked up her bra and aimed his light down the stone steps. Her pink, lacy panties lay on the bottom step.

"Very cute, Meg."

The thought of her waiting naked gave him an instant erection. His wife could be so mischievous when she wanted sex.

"Okay, Squeaky, you win." Casey started down the steps, which were flat river stones, crudely masoned into an uneven staircase. Lichen grew over them, slickening his descent. A couple of eroded stones loosened from their mortar seals, tilting as he stepped on them. He slipped once, catching the wall to keep from falling on his ass.

The cellar smelled earthy, like a creek after a heavy rain. At the bottom was a dirt floor. White mushrooms clustered in the corner. Casey's hiking shoes sank into damp, black soil that hadn't seen sunlight in over a century. He saw fingers moving in the dirt, and his breath caught in his throat. It was an illusion brought on by a sudden fear. The fingers were actually earthworms poking their heads out to observe this giant intruder.

Casey stepped over them and ventured into the gloom. There was a chill down here that prickled his skin. A few cold drops dripped onto his neck and rolled down his back, making him shiver. Tilting his headlamp up, Casey saw beads of dampness clinging to the ceiling. The wood overhead was covered in a skin of black mold. Spores of the stuff floated in the air; he inhaled them, tasted the blight on his tongue. Another drop of moisture struck his forehead and ran stickily down his cheek. He wiped away the scourge and moved on, eager to find his bare-skinned nymph.

The basement was as pitch-black as any underground cave. Impossible to tell how far it went. The more he pressed, the more he kept finding dark upon dark. There seemed to be nothing down here except dirt and mushrooms and moss-covered walls. The deeper Casey walked, his mind kept going back to the witches who had vanished in this house. *They found the decapitated heads mounted on sticks, but never found their bodies,* Ronnie had said.

Casey took each step carefully, watching the dirt floor for movement. Another question burrowed at the back of his brain: If all the cult members were murdered, who killed them? Abigail Blackwood, all by herself? Impossible. Then who?

No one, answered his rational mind. *They all dropped too much acid and killed each other.*

That explanation calmed Casey's nerves a bit. When he got twenty feet under the house, he began to worry about Meg. This was so unlike her to tease him for so long. And why the hell would she want to come down here naked anyhow? She boggled his mind sometimes. "Meg, I'm tired of playing hide-and-seek. Will you come out already?"

Her headlamp flashed on in the distance.

Casey released a sigh of relief. "There you are." He walked toward her and felt his nerves twitch when he noticed her light was at ground level. Something passed in front of the beam of light, causing it to flicker briefly. Casey made out Meg's moving bare feet and her pale-white buttocks, as she danced in a circle around her caving helmet. Her gyrations were fluid, tribal, not like Meg at all. As much as he loved her, the girl had no rhythm. Except now, she danced with gypsy grace, which made him wonder again if she was on something.

"Meg, whatever you're doing, this isn't funny."

She laughed, mocking him, and kept dancing and fluttering, round and round.

As he approached within ten feet, she turned toward him, swaying her hips and moving her arms in front of her like serpents. A wagging finger beckoned him to come to her.

The sight of his wife's exposed sex and breasts aroused him again, but Casey was too angry with her games now to welcome the invitation. "No, I'm not going any farther," he protested. "You come here."

She danced forward, her face entering the light from his helmet. Casey gasped. Meg's eyes were full of black ooze, with a sharp prong poking outward from each socket. A third prong jutted from her mouth, moving it up and down, pantomiming laughter. A hollow doll's giggle issued from her throat. As Casey's eyes adjusted, he saw black vines twined around her arms and legs, controlling her like a marionette.

"Oh, fuck..." Casey folded to his knees, his jaw trembling. Urine dampened his crotch.

His mind turned to jelly, unable to fathom what he was seeing. Meg looked dead, yet she was moving. And then he realized stalks were connected to an animated darkness behind her. A mass of unknown size was undulating beyond the halo of their lights. He heard the sounds of roots ripping from the earth. More black vines snaked around Meg's body. Coiled around her breasts. Thorny prongs poked through her skin, tainting it with red.

"No!" he shouted, reaching for her.

In one sudden motion, the vines tore Meg apart. An explosion of liquid, flesh and bone splattered against Casey's face and shirt.

"Oh God!" He stumbled backward.

Something in the black chasm screamed like an enraged woman. The earth shuddered as it advanced.

The soil shifted under Casey's feet. Roots sprouted upward, curling over his shoes.

He turned tail and ran.

The abomination chased him, releasing a roar that was less woman and more animal.

Casey's caving helmet shook side to side as he ran. Above him, rivers of black sludge flowed across the ceiling. Along the walls the mushrooms shook. Whatever the thing down here was, the fungus was a part of it.

He reached the cellar steps, stumbling up the slippery stones. A beam of light jabbed into Casey's eyes.

At the top of the stairs stood Ronnie, holding a flashlight.

The beast shrieked from the darkness at Casey's back.

"Help!" He scampered up the final steps.

"You ain't nothing but meat now." Ronnie slammed the door.

Casey pounded against it. "Let me out! Let me out!"

It was at the bottom of the steps now, making guttural noises, filling the air with pungent spores.

And then came the vines, squirming up Casey's pants, tearing through his shirt, into his flesh, around his throat. He fought against the wooden tentacles as he was pulled down the steps and into the horror's widening jaws.

10

It was happening again. Otis woke up when he heard the screams inside his head. People inside his house. Damned trespassers. He dropped his bottle of whiskey. Balled his hand into a fist and hit his skull, the way Grandpa used to hit him when he got to drinking.

The Blevins house flashed moving pictures in Otis's head, like scenes from a horror film. He saw the violence of the young couple in the cellar. The girl torn apart. The bloody flesh and bones of the boy being broken down into pulp. The earthworms squirming for the blood and meaty morsels that fell to the dirt. Inside the house, Mama's appetite was growing. She smelled fresh food.

Otis saw the others up in the attic, prying through his things, going through his scrapbook.

Mama was upset now, her rage expanding through the walls of the house.

Otis couldn't tolerate this happening. Not one damned bit. Scooting from the table, he grabbed his shotgun and headed to the truck. He peeled down the road with Mama's anger burning hot inside his head.

11

Dean shook the attic door. "It's stuck."

"Ronnie locked it," Sarah insisted.

"Why would he do that?"

"I don't know. He's *your* friend."

"He wouldn't lock us in on purpose," Dean argued. "The door's stuck."

"You can be so bullheaded," she snapped.

"Yeah, well, at the first challenge, you're ready to bolt. You almost jerked me off my feet."

She fidgeted with the rope. "Maybe you should unleash me then."

Dean crossed his arms. "We're staying tied together."

They glared at one another in a standoff. Their first big fight. And, she feared, their last. She paced.

"Sarah, calm down."

"I'll calm down when we're outside. Right now I'm pissed. Why would Ronnie leave us up here?"

"I don't know. Maybe he went outside to take a leak. Let's chill up here till he gets back."

"I don't want to wait. I want out of this house *now*." She was sounding like a frightened child, and she hated herself for it, but they were in danger. She could feel it in her bones.

Dean put his arms around Sarah and held her shaking body. "I'm here with you. You're safe."

She looked him in the eyes. "If you want me to feel safe, then don't blow off my concerns."

"Okay, I'm sorry. Let's stop fighting." Dean waved his hands, calling a truce. "I'll keep trying." He shoved his shoulder into the door with another heroic effort, then started pounding. "Maybe Casey and Meg will hear us and come up." He yelled their names and continued hammering the wood with his fist. When no one responded, he stopped, looking frustrated.

"What about the tools we found?" Sarah asked. "We can break the knob off."

"I'm not ready to go to that extreme just yet. I'd feel bad if we damaged the owner's property when we didn't have to. Let's look for another door."

"Fine. As long as we're doing something." She followed him through the shadowy maze of antiques. The plastic draping lifted upward as they passed. Sarah thought she glimpsed someone crouched off to her left. A swish of her flashlight identified the headless sewing mannequin. She saw the crate of dusty tools and picked up a claw hammer.

Dean gave her a look and she shot him one back. Sarah would put the hammer back when she was done with it, but right now she needed the comfort of a weapon in her hand. If Ronnie suddenly sprang from beneath the plastic, Sarah was going to nail him.

Dean's machismo must have kicked in, because he dug into his backpack and pulled out a tool that he'd brought—a hammer-hatchet combination.

Something made a noise up above. They both jerked their flashlights upward. Some birds roosting up in the rafters. Sarah was so on edge she laughed.

Then she saw the ropes.

Every few feet lengths of old rope were knotted to the crossbeams. They dangled down a foot or so, the ends shredded. She thought of the six people who had hung themselves up here. But there were more than just six knots of broken rope. Dozens. And some of the rope looked new.

On the far side of the stored heirlooms, the attic opened up to a stretch of empty space. There was some light at the far end, thanks to a hole in the clapboards. Sarah could see a little blue sky through it, and she suddenly yearned to be in the sun. In the gray gloom she saw just how wide the attic was, at least twenty feet across. They separated, moving toward opposite walls. The tether between them stretched, causing them to play tug-of-war. Dean let out more slack.

On one side of the attic, Sarah searched the stone wall for a hidden doorway. *Please be one of those houses that has a second set of stairs to the attic.* The ancient stones were covered in more of that nasty black mold. It tainted the air she inhaled. Did it just move? She had the impression that when she passed the light over the wall, the fungus shifted, like a snake coiling. The dark was messing with her eyes. Along the bottom of the wall, she found etchings in the stones—symbols like the ones they found painted in the ceremonial room downstairs. These hieroglyphs looked older than old, as if she were exploring a Druid temple.

"Dean, I found some more markings in the rock."

"They're on this side too. Engraved on every brick. Weird."

Sarah followed the etchings, wondering who'd carved them. She nearly reached the back wall when the floor made a *creaking* sound, and then a louder *crack*. Then the floor was gone, and she was falling into darkness.

12

Dean heard the shattering of brittle wood and Sarah's scream. The rope between them snapped taut. Yanked him off his feet. He slid across the attic floor toward a gaping hole. On impulse, he chopped the hatchet into the floorboards. The blade stuck. He slid to a halt, the recoil almost dislocating his shoulder. The rapid plunging of his girlfriend's fall twisted his body around.

His eyes followed the rope that went over the edge. "Sarah!"

"Help!" She sounded so far away. "Dean, get me out of here!"

"Are you hurt?"

Several scary seconds went by before she answered. "No, but I'm stuck in midair."

"Hold on, Sarah. I'm going to pull you up."

With one hand still gripping the hatchet, his other hand struggled to pull up the rope. Without leverage, he could barely lift it an inch. He gasped.

Think, Dean, think!

The rope, carabiners and harnesses were top-brand rock-climbing gear designed to handle falls from mountain cliffs. As long as Dean didn't let go of the hatchet, Sarah wouldn't fall any farther.

His arm and shoulder hurt like a motherfucker. His palm was sweating.

He needed leverage. He spotted a round hole in one of the floorboards and got an idea.

* * *

Sarah dangled in the darkness. She had fallen into one of the bedrooms on the second floor. Down below her, the floor was covered in piles of ceiling plaster and broken boards with rusty nails. The remaining drop was only five or six feet, but she was stuck in her harness and didn't know how to get out of the damned thing. Every time she moved, her body swung, and the fraying rope dragged across the sharp edge of the broken wood above. She prayed the line didn't snap.

She had dropped the hammer and her flashlight, which winked out. The only light now came from her helmet. She heard chirring noises coming from somewhere in the house. Thumps and creaking wood. Footsteps up a staircase? Someone was moving about. She jerked her beam to the open doorway. The hall was a black void, as if beyond the room was eternal nothingness. The house turned quiet again, and that was more unnerving than the noises.

Sarah was surprised that Casey and Meg hadn't come running at the sound of the crash. Where were they? She considered calling for them. But what if Ronnie came instead? Sarah shuddered and switched off her light. She didn't want to call attention to herself. She hung there, waiting on her knight in shining armor to pull her up. The gaping hole above was visible from the glow of Dean's helmet light. Sarah could hear him hammering up there.

In between knocks against wood, she heard squishing sounds within the bedroom.

She switched on her light. The black fungus on the walls had definitely moved. No, impossible. She panned her light around the room. The walls and ceiling were covered with the mold. It glistened as if water was seeping through the walls. Sarah felt like she was in a damp cave. The room even smelled subterranean. From one splotch on the ceiling, slime hung in threads of drool and sloughed off, splatting against the floor.

Sarah clung to the rope. "Dean, please pull me up."

* * *

Sweat dripped off Dean's face as he worked with one free hand. He had used his knife to chisel a small hole between the floorboards. Then he stuck a cam inside the crevice and opened the metal teeth, locking it in place. From his backpack, he fished out a quickdraw and hooked one of the carabiners to the cam. He gave it a quick yank. It held. The boards he lay on seemed to be stronger than the flooring where Sarah had fallen through. Trusting this assumption, he clamped the quickdraw's second carabiner onto his harness and loosened his grip on the hatchet. The cam groaned between the boards, but maintained its hold.

Dean released the hatchet handle and sat up. He gripped the rope with both hands and started pulling with all the leverage he could muster. The weight of Sarah's hanging body was too much to lift from his position. He needed to get closer to the hole. Using his hatchet and a second set of cams and quickdraws, he worked a new line of rope and crawled on his belly to the hole. Parts of the floor were soft as mulch. The boards *creaked* beneath him. He peered over the edge.

Hanging in midair, Sarah looked up at him.

Dean almost cried at the sight of her. "You all right?"

"Just scared shitless."

"I've secured the rope."

"Can you pull me up?"

"I'm thinking it would be better if I lowered you. I don't trust this flooring."

"Okay. Please hurry."

Adjusting his belay, he slowly began easing her down. She was almost to the bottom when Dean heard footsteps behind him. He turned in time to see a board swinging towards his head.

13

Sarah's shoes almost touched the ground, but she was halted by a sudden jerking of the rope. Above, Dean was no longer at the hole's edge. His light swished wildly in the attic, and Sarah could hear sounds of a struggle. He yelled and then went silent.

"Dean!?"

Several agonizing seconds passed.

"Dean, answer me!"

Ronnie leaned over the edge, grinning down at her. "Howdy."

"Where's Dean?"

"Your boyfriend's out of commission." Ronnie wiped blood from the corner of his mouth. In his other hand, he was holding a knife. "You hang there a moment while I finish my business. I'll be down for you soon." He moved out of sight.

Sarah yelled for Dean again, but he still didn't answer. Panicking, she screamed for Casey and Meg.

"Stop making so much racket." Ronnie returned to the hole in the ceiling. "You're just wasting your breath. Your friends won't be coming."

"Where are they?"

"They're worm food down in the cellar. It's just us now, little piggy. You, me and Mama. And she's gonna be real happy to meet you." The lunatic disappeared into the darkness.

Sarah dangled like a marionette, only the toes of her shoes touching the floor. She fought against the harness, but couldn't get out of it. If only she had a knife to cut the line. Her only hope was unclamping where her harness was hooked onto the rope. She squeezed the carabiner's gate open, but her weight pulled down on the cord, preventing her from unhooking it. Panic rose in her chest.

Breathe, Sarah, breathe. She took a deep breath and exhaled. The panic subsided and the solution came to her instantly. She began scaling the rope, using all her strength to pull herself up. She unhooked the carabiner and dropped to the floor, landing on her feet. There was no time to feel victorious. She picked up her hammer and switched off her helmet lamp.

From down the hall, she could hear Ronnie singing an old country tune.

* * *

Ronnie danced in the hallway as he whistled the song and peered into the bedrooms. He loved the thrill of the hunt. Sometimes he'd let his prey loose in the house just to play hide-and-seek with them. Mama said their meat tasted better when their blood was pumping with fear. The ugly chicks he always delivered straight to the cellar. The pretty ones, though, he liked to play Hump the Hog with. Male, female, it didn't matter. A pig was a pig. He got a hard-on just thinking about his prey on all fours. His semen inside their bodies added a salty flavor to Mama's meal.

Now which room was piggy in? He stabbed his light into each doorway he passed. The rooms without closets offered no place to hide, except behind the doors. Ronnie always checked there first. He was a skilled hunter.

He observed the shifting fungus on all the walls. Mama was getting impatient. If he didn't bring her supper soon, she was going to take matters into her own hands. Ronnie had seen her angry and knew best not to be in the house when she lost her temper. He might be the bastard son of a witch, but he was made of the same substance as the meals he brought her.

"Oh, piggy..." he whistled for her, "...here piggy, piggy..."

* * *

Sarah crouched in the pitch-dark of the bedroom. Ronnie's footsteps and whistling were growing closer. She clamped her jaw shut, holding her breath, trying not to make a sound. Her body wouldn't stop shaking. She felt the urge to pee, but held that in too.

She could hear the fungus moving along the walls and ceiling. It dripped into puddles on the wood floor. She imagined a giant black amoeba oozing toward her, coating her body in slime, eating her flesh. When it slithered away, she imagined being nothing but a skeleton holding the hammer, waiting for her killer to discover the fungus had beaten him to the punch.

The twisted vision was broken by the approach of a

flashlight. "Where ya hidin', piggy? I know you're in one of these rooms."

Her heart beat faster. It sounded like thunder in the room. Could Ronnie hear it too?

She considered hiding behind the door, but sensed he would look there, jabbing his light into the crack. She would be trapped. Instead, she hovered in the corner next to the open doorway.

His light beam poked into the room. An arm crossed the threshold. The side of his face. Sarah pounced. Struck him with the hammer.

Ronnie fell to the floor, grabbing his head. "You bitch!"

She ran past him. A hand caught her ankle and she tumbled.

He crawled toward her. She kicked his face. Ripped loose from his hands and ran into the hallway. His light switched off behind her.

The dark closed in around her.

Her hand touched a wall and slid through its slickness. The mildew assaulted her senses. Something rumbled down in the bowels of the house.

Never-ending darkness.

Which direction was she running? Where was the attic? Where was Dean?

Please, be alive!

She switched on her headlamp. Saw the banister, the stairway leading down.

Wrong way. The attic was behind her.

And so was Ronnie. Charging from the shadows. Blood streaming down his maniacal face. He growled. "Come back here!"

Sarah ran down the stairs, two at a time. The front door to her right, precious sunlight blooming around the edges.

The doorway to freedom.

At the bottom of the stairs, Ronnie tackled her. They rolled across the floor. The walls and ceiling spun. The hammer slid out of her hand. And then he was on top of her, wrapping rope around her wrists. Sarah jerked and kicked as he dragged her across the stone floor.

14

Otis parked his truck on the side of the dirt road. His head shook violently as he felt what was happening inside the house. He pounded his fist on the dashboard. "No, no, no, no!"

Ronnie Blevins was doing bad things again.

"Damn it, that boy!" Otis regretted the day he saved his baby brother from Mama's wrath.

When the spasms stopped, Otis wiped spittle off his chin. He blubbered, not knowing what to do.

"Please don't cry, Little Otie," his mama said.

Otis turned to see Mama's ghost sitting in the cab beside him. She was wearing that flowered dress she always wore on hot summer days. The one that clung to her body.

"I don't wanna hurt nobody, Mama."

She put her hand on his face. "I know you don't, sweetie, but I need to feed in order to survive. You want Mama to stay alive, don't you?"

Otis nodded, sniffling. He thought of all the good times they had shared when he was a little boy. He remembered his last night with her over forty years ago. He and his pig Jasper had gone down into the cellar to take Mama her evening meal. For two weeks she had been chained to a wall. The Pit of Darkness was where people stayed when they had the demon in them. As soon as the person calmed down and became obedient, they could come out and rejoin the coven. But Mama seemed to be growing crazier. He could hear her talking to herself in the darkness.

He searched with a flashlight. "Mama, you okay?"

"Little Otie?" She looked like a filthy animal when she crawled toward him. Black soil covered every inch of her. She pulled Otis into her arms. "Oh, baby, I've missed you so much."

"I missed you too."

"Are they treating you okay up there?"

"Uh huh."

"How's Baby Ronnie?"

"He cries in his crib a lot." Otis's little brother was only two years old.

Mama's face turned angry. "Who's in charge now?"

"Abigail. She can be so mean. She makes me do chores all day."

"Well, when I come back out, I won't make you do any more chores."

"Good. 'Cause I don't like 'em." He held up a bucket. "Brought you some dinner."

"Thank you, sweetie." She devoured the meat and potatoes that Abigail had thrown into the bucket like slops. She had told Otis, "Go feed your pig."

After Mama ate, she guzzled down the bottle of water.

Otis said, "I have to go back upstairs now."

"No, stay with me, Otie. I made a little hidey-hole for us." She crawled over to a hole she'd dug under a shelf where they stored fruit jars. He crawled down into the burrow and lay with Mama. She wrapped her arms around him and sang in her sweet voice. *"Dheannain sùgradh ris a nighean duibh … N'deidh dhomh eirigh as a 'mhadainn…"*

When the Gaelic song was over, she asked, "Did I ever tell you the legend of Nyraena the Underworld Witch?"

Otis shook his head. "Is she magical like you and Grammy?"

"Even more so. Thousands of years ago, Nyraena was one of Pan's wood nymphs until she one day denied him her love. Pan got so angry that he and his coven of nymphs imprisoned Nyraena in a cavern deep within the earth. Pan wanted her to die a lonely death."

"Did she die?" Otis asked.

"No, she survived by eating cave mushrooms, roots and worms, and licking spores and lichen off the stones." Mama gently rocked Otis. "Spending all those centuries living underground, Nyraena began to change, like how a caterpillar in a cocoon becomes a moth. When her metamorphosis was complete, she turned into a powerful Underworld Witch and now reigns over all creatures living inside the soil."

"Like worms and bugs?"

"Yes, Otie, and the roots and mushrooms too. Nyraena had one problem, though. She was painfully lonely in her cave. And the anger she had for Pan and the other nymphs would never leave. Sometimes, when you put your ear to the ground, you can hear Nyraena's cries."

Otis listened, but didn't hear anything except the hum from the generator.

Mama said, "I've been hearing her a lot lately. Nyraena wants me to set her free from her prison. In exchange, she promises to help me take back the coven." She pulled him tight against her chest. "I'm going to set the Underworld Witch free, Otie. And I need your help."

15

Sarah struggled with the bindings that tied her wrists to the rails at the bottom of the stairs. She carefully watched Ronnie, who was across the hall, pacing in the shadows of the ceremonial room. He was talking to someone, but Sarah could only see half the den from her angle. Was there another person with him? And were Meg and Casey really dead?

The thought tore at Sarah's heart. She hadn't begun to accept the loss of Dean. Just this morning the four of them had been laughing together over breakfast, talking about today's adventure. Now Dean, Meg and Casey were gone, and Sarah was alone in an abandoned house with a crazed redneck. She wept. She hadn't told anyone she was coming here. Her parents would never know what happened to their daughter. Just gone. Vanished without a trace. Sarah thought of her dog, Bandit, standing at the front window, wondering when she was going to return and take him to the park.

Sarah sobbed so hard her chest hurt.

"Get the tears out," her kickboxing coached had yelled into her ear the first time he pushed her further than she wanted to go. *"After the tears, you'll unleash your anger.*

And that's where your power comes from." That day she had kicked the bag with a ferocity she didn't know she had in her.

Now her tears subsided and the rage came quickly. She wasn't ready to die. She yanked at the ropes.

"What do ya think you're doing?" Ronnie stepped back into the circle of light.

"Stay away from me!"

"Piggy, you and I are just gettin' started." He unbuckled his jeans, unzipped. "I'm gonna make you oink so loud." He got down on all fours and crawled toward her.

Sarah kicked him in the face. He backed up, shocked by the assault.

"Don't touch me," Sarah warned. "Or I'll kick your teeth in." Her anger shrouded her fear. She sat against the banister with her leg cocked, ready to strike another blow.

Ronnie wiped blood from his busted lip and grinned. "You're a feisty little piggy. After I hog-fuck ya, I'm gonna corn ya too."

He lunged. Sarah kicked his shoulder, but he didn't stop. He wrapped his arms around her legs, flipped her over. Sarah struggled, but Ronnie was too strong. He grappled her from behind. His erection poked through his jeans.

"Sooie!" He laughed and slapped her thigh and made oinking sounds.

"No!" she screamed and bucked against him.

He pressed a blade against her throat. "Stop moving or I'll gut you."

She sobbed as he sliced off her harness and tossed it aside. His hands fumbled to unbuckle her shorts.

"Please stop!" Sarah pleaded.

Something flashed in the darkness, lighting up the den briefly. Then Sarah heard a woman's cry that sounded like an enraged banshee.

Ronnie backed away with a frightened look on his face. He walked into the darkness. "Mama, I was gonna bring her to you when I was done."

Sarah searched for the woman who had made the sound. Sarah heard no response, but Ronnie kept talking anyway. "Please, let me have her first!"

Something ungodly roared from the far corner of the house. Then came a pounding on the door.

Ronnie stepped back into the circle of light, buckling his pants. He looked terrified. "You're meat now, piggy." He pushed his nose up like a snout. "Oink, oink." Then he hurried down the hall to the front door.

Sarah saw a fleeting second of sunlight and then the door shut. The *click* of a lock destroyed her last hope of escape. Like all the other victims before her, she too would die here and forever haunt this godforsaken house.

16

June 1972

While everyone in the coven was sleeping, six-year-old Otis collected all the things that Mama had asked for and brought them down to the cellar. Her chains rattled as she crawled toward him and took the burlap sack from his hands. "Good boy." She opened a spell book and frantically turned the pages.

Otis dug through the sack and pulled out a knife and a jar filled with hair, fingernail clippings and teeth.

"What are these for?" Otis asked.

"My mama, your grammy, taught me to always collect hair and nails from those around you, because you never know when your friends will become your enemies." She held up a thick bundle of black hair. "Oh, Abigail, you're going to regret ever crossing me." Mama dropped the hair into a bowl-shaped hole in the ground. She poured out all the contents in the jar. Then she dug into the burlap sack and pulled out a human skull.

Otis shrank back. "What's that for?"

"A skull has great power in it. Especially one from a witch, and your grammy was an even more powerful conjurer than me." Mama set his grandmother's skull on top of the pile of hair and fingernails.

With the knife, she sliced open her hand and sprinkled her blood over everything in the hole.

"Now, I need your pig."

"Not Jasper."

"Otie, sometimes the gods and goddesses require us to give sacrifices. A spell is even more powerful when you offer them something you love. You want Mama to be free, don't you?"

The boy nodded. He hugged Jasper one last time, then handed him over. The piglet squealed and wriggled in Mama's arms. Otis cried as she cut its throat. She poured Jasper's blood over Grammy's skull, then set the pig's dead body in the hole. Then Mama buried the contents for her spell and placed her palms on the dirt. "I invoke thee, Nyraena, the Terrible and Invisible Witch who dwelleth in the darkest void of the earth. Whose suffering is my suffering. Whose glory is my glory. I offer you these gifts."

Mama scooped up the bloody soil and wiped it on her face. "Hear me, Nyraena, and make all spirits subject unto me, so that every spirit of the Firmament and of the Ether, upon the earth and under the earth. And every scourge of my coven, and anyone who dare cross me, may be obedient to me. *Arogorobra Sothou!*"

Otis and Mama waited in silence for a long moment. Then he felt the ground rumble. The walls began to shudder and the pipes above their heads rattled. He crawled backward as Mama started shaking violently. Her eyes rolled back to whites. Her mouth opened wide and hordes of spiders crawled from her throat, skittering across her face. And then roots started coming out of the ground. They snaked around her body, shredding her clothes, covering her in a cocoon of roots, dirt and earthworms, until all he could see were the solid whites of Mama's eyes.

Otis ran away screaming.

* * *

Now, Otis looked at Mama's ghost sitting in the truck next to him, as pretty as when he was a kid. "You promised to take me with you to our special hidey-hole, but you left me behind with Grandpa and Ronnie."

"I needed you to take care of the house and look after your baby brother."

After the police found Otis and two-year-old Ronnie still alive, the two boys had gone to live with their grandpa on the pig farm.

"Grandpa was always drunk and mean. He hurt me and Ronnie."

"And I stopped Grandpa from beating you, didn't I?"

Otis wiped snot on his sleeve and nodded, remembering the day Grandpa walked into the pigsty with his shotgun and blew off half his own head. The pigs had themselves a feast that day.

Now Mama smiled and pinched Otis's cheek. "So why don't you go on home? Let Ronnie handle the feeding tonight."

Something flickered in his mama's eyes. An evil he had never seen there before. The mama he remembered had always looked at him with kind eyes. But after she merged with Nyraena and slaughtered the coven, Mama had changed. First, she wanted him to sacrifice his dear pigs to the house so she could feed. Then when her hunger grew, she began to ask for human meat. When Otis refused, Mama started getting close to Ronnie.

Otis had tried to teach his younger brother right from wrong. Had shown him how to feed pigs to the house so Mama stayed fed. But Ronnie had a weak will when it came to Mama. Now he was killing more people.

"This has got to stop," Otis shouted. "This can't go on no more."

Her ghost leaned over for a kiss, and he backed away. "Sorry, Mama. I hope you'll forgive me." Gripping his shotgun, he climbed out of his truck and hiked into the woods.

"Otie, come back!"

He tried to be strong and brave, but the sound of his mama crying brought Otis to tears.

Part Three

The Cellar Beast

17

Dean woke up in a fuzzy haze, groaning. *Where am I?*

His eyes adjusted to the gloom. A flock of birds flew down from the rafters and out a hole in the boarded window. He sat up, head aching. Tried to move his hands and legs, but they were bound at the wrists and ankles by climbing rope.

"What the fuck?"

And then it all came back to him—Ronnie blindsiding him. The two of them rolling around on the floor throwing punches. *Fucking bastard.* Dean's heart raced as he realized he'd left Sarah hanging. Her rope still dangled over the edge. "Sarah!"

No response.

Dean flipped on his helmet light and inch-wormed over to the hole and peered down. The end of the rope was empty. He yelled, "Sarah!"

* * *

Sarah lifted her tear-soaked face up from her hands and looked toward the distant voice.

"Dean!?"

He called her name again from above. *Yes, alive!*

"I'm tied up downstairs!" she yelled back, crying hopeful tears now.

She could hear him trying to communicate, but the words were muffled. She thought she understood the last three words—"coming for you."

"I'm on the ground floor, Dean! Please hurry!"

They were going to make it somehow. Any moment, Dean would come and untie her. They would break down the front door together and escape.

Again, pounding echoed from the far end of the house on the ground floor, where the kitchen was located. And then a horrible thought struck Sarah. A woman was pounding behind the cellar door. Meg—alive somehow? But this woman's cries didn't sound human.

18

Up in the attic, Dean had been slicing the wrist ropes with his hatchet blade when the whole house shuddered. The wood groaned. The stones in the walls rippled with a sound like falling dominoes. All the symbols etched in the bricks began to glow.

Dean released a breath, awestruck by the miracle he was seeing.

The garret became alive with skittering sounds. The black mold appeared to be migrating across the walls like armies of marching ants. Something sticky hit his neck. He tilted his light up to the vaulted ceiling. Spindles of dark drool oozed down in several places, forming into what looked like black cocoons. As the slime kept sliding down, building upon itself, the glistening cocoons shaped into people's bodies hanging from the rafters. Directly in front of him, one of the fungus-covered ghosts vaguely resembled Abigail Blackwood.

"Holy shit." At the sound of Dean's voice the heads twisted on their broken necks, looking down at him.

* * *

In the ceremonial room downstairs, the circle of candles caught flame, illuminating the bowl of animal bones. The symbols the witches had chalked on the walls glimmered with orange light.

Sarah gasped. From every direction she heard wet, squelching sounds. On walls, floors, ceilings, the black mold slid across the surfaces, congealing into large fungal masses. In several places, the dark matter pooled on the floor and began rising. It looked like swamp trees growing in fast motion. Around the glowing circle, the tree branches shaped into human arms, the trunks into legs—a coven of nude women covered in mold and slime. Old hags, beautiful apprentices and obese women were among the coven. Their seated bodies swayed before a large-breasted woman standing in the center. She held up the severed head of a goat.

In the kitchen, the cellar door burst open with a shriek.

Sarah struggled to unknot the bindings on her wrists. Violent images flashed in her mind…women screaming as they were being torn apart in the ceremonial room… another woman running down the hallway…another drowning her children in a bathtub. Six people hanging themselves in the attic, their necks snapping. The final image made her cry—Dean hanging by a noose.

"No!" Sarah pulled at the rope. Growling, she leaned back and kicked at the rails.

The ghosts of the witches rose to their feet. Their heads craned together, staring at Sarah. Down the hall, the floorboards buckled. Multiple arms and tentacles sprouted from the darkness, scraping the walls and ceiling.

Sarah kicked again and again. The rail snapped, broke loose from the banister. She slid the ropes off and looked back at the ceremonial room. The coven of shadows began walking toward her. Behind them moved a dark mass that filled the hallway. The thing from the cellar shrieked again with an angry, guttural voice.

Sarah screamed and ran up the stairs.

On the second floor, she raced down the long hallway. "Dean!"

A man's ghost stepped in front of the attic door. He stretched out an arm that dripped with muck. He walked toward Sarah, like a man freshly dug from the grave. Behind him, more dark specters stepped out of the rooms.

Sarah backpedaled.

Behind her, the witches were coming up the stairs.

She darted into a bathroom and closed the door. The tiled floors and walls were speckled with that hideous, slithering blight. Along the back wall sat a claw-foot bathtub filled to the brim with black water. Sarah shook uncontrollably as the wood floors in the hallway creaked beneath several feet. The worst of the sounds were the moans.

She shut off her light. In pitch-dark, she held the knob, her whole body trembling. Wet slaps against the door. It pushed open an inch. Sarah put all her weight against the door, shoved it closed again. Fumbling around the knob, she found a lock and bolted it.

She fell back against the door and released a breath.

In the darkness, the water in the tub splashed.

19

The ghosts aren't really there, Dean tried to convince himself as he cut the last of his bindings. Either the dark was playing tricks on his eyes or Ronnie had set up some kind of hologram machine to create the illusion. There was no time to appreciate the spectacle.

Dean picked up the hatchet and slipped his backpack on. He considered retrieving his cams and quickdraws and the rope dangling over the hole in the floor, but there was no time. He had to get out of this attic and find Sarah. There was only one exit and it was at the opposite end. He'd chop the goddamned door down if he had to.

The hanging ghosts rocked the crossbeams above him, their feet swinging. He counted over a dozen men and women. Some were dressed in '70s clothing; others—teenagers and college students—wore more recent clothes. Their bulging eyes kept looking at him. They all shifted and struggled against the ropes around their necks.

The symbols flashed bright again. Dean's head rocked back as it was filled with screams and moving pictures—Sarah running through the house…the face of a wretched creature down in the cellar…the witches carrying his dear Sarah away…

He heard her screaming his name downstairs.

"Sarah!" he yelled for her.

When Dean opened his eyes, the ghosts were no longer hanging above him. He turned to see a crowd had gathered behind him. Abigail Blackwood smiled and held up a noose.

* * *

At the sound of splashing water, Sarah turned on her helmet light.

In the bathtub, a nude woman was rising out of the black scum. She stretched out her arms and wailed with a gargling voice.

Sarah screamed and flattened against the door.

The slime-covered woman fumbled over the edge of the tub. Smacked the tile floor. Crawling on her belly, she lashed out and gripped Sarah's ankle with a cold, wet hand. Sarah kicked her foot through the ghost's head, and her body collapsed into a puddle.

In the bathtub, two more heads emerged from the soup. Their bodies rose.

Sarah yanked a towel bar off the wall and swung at their heads. With each strike, the water ghosts burst, falling back into the broth, but more heads kept bubbling up. The heads of children.

Sarah yelped and backed away. Something thumped against her helmet. Above, an arm had grown out of a patch of black fungus. Its hand swooped at her, grazing her cheek. Other arms stretched out from the walls. The dead children rising out of the tub stepped onto the tile, little arms reaching for hugs from Mommy. Too many of them now.

She opened the door and fled into the bedroom. Her helmet light passed across hideous faces in the dark. Hands groped for her. Sarah knocked them away with the towel bar and ran back into the hall. The passage to the attic was clogged with moving bodies. The ghosts moaned, moving toward her. She bolted in the opposite direction. "Dean!"

He screamed from above, "Sarah!"

She found the room where she'd fallen through the ceiling. "Dean!"

His head peered over the edge. "Run, Sarah! Get out of the hou—"

A noose wrapped around his neck. Several hands jerked him away.

She screamed for him. She had to save him. The wood floor creaked behind her. She turned and saw the ghosts of the witches pouring into the room.

Sarah backed into a corner, fighting off their slimy hands. The eyes in their fungus-covered skulls were dark, empty holes. Sarah gouged the cheeks of the woman with ample breasts, her hand passing right through the thin veil of flesh. The dead women were ghostly shells made from the scum of the house, yet they had strength. They pulled Sarah into the crowd, moaning and groping her face and body. She clawed and kicked as they lifted her above their heads and carried her out of the room. She cried as they took her downstairs, towards the kitchen. By the time the ghosts stepped into the cellar, Sarah had passed out from terror.

20

Dean slid on his back across the attic floor as the lynch mob dragged him with a rope. He had slipped his hand between his neck and the noose a split second before they cinched it. It tightened around his hand, cutting off the blood, but he kept the cord high against his chin to keep from choking.

They stopped dragging him. He watched in horror as a tall ghost flung the rope over one of the crossbeams. The others, still wearing their own severed nooses, watched the hangman prepare the gallows.

Dean felt along his hip and found his hunting knife still in its sheath.

The hangman pulled on the rope, lifting Dean painfully to his feet. He sawed at the rope above his head. Another yank and he was up on his toes now, the cord squeezing his hand against his throat. Choking. The mob spun him like a piñata.

As the executioner pulled Dean off his feet, the blade cut the rope and he fell to the floor, gasping for air. Hands grabbed him. He sliced at the crowd with the knife. He broke loose from their hold and ran across the attic. Retrieved his hatchet. The horde of shadows walked toward him, moaning. The light from the symbols glowing in the walls lit up their hideous, mold-covered faces.

Gripping the hatchet and knife, Dean chopped their heads, slit their throats. Those ghosts lost cohesion and disintegrated into puffs of floating spores. But more of the walking-mold people filled their places, grabbing his arms and shoulders.

"Get back!" Swinging the blades, lopping off hands and fingers, he backed up to the far wall, where the broken boards covered the window.

Abigail Blackwood approached, a wicked grin on her leprous face. Giggling, she held up another noose. The tall hangman walked behind her, tossing another cord over a beam. At the window behind Dean, a ray of sunlight lanced through the hole in one corner. When the witch girl stepped into it, the sunbeam burned her chest. Abigail screamed as she flared up and the mold that held her together burst away like fleeing fireflies.

Alarmed, the other ghosts stopped five feet away.

"Fear the sun, do you?" Dean chopped at the window boards with the hatchet, widening the hole to the outside world. More sunbeams speared into the loft, burning the crowd. The hangman exploded into embers. The others backed away, wailing in fear.

Dean kept chopping the boards, kicking off larger planks, until half the attic was washed in glorious sunlight. More ghosts collapsed. Some ran into the shadows where the antiques were stored. Others disappeared into the stone walls, leaving behind black stains. Even the fungus on the bricks retreated to the dark end of the attic.

Dean caught his breath. Wiped sweat off his face.

Through the open window, he could see the forest outside. The orange sun was low on the horizon, approaching dusk. He didn't want to be in this house after dark.

He needed to search for Sarah. He remembered the visions of the ghosts carrying her away. He knew in his gut they had taken her to the cellar, where the witch-beast lived. He could feel the creature in his head now, worming through his brain. The invasion into his thoughts and fears connected his mind to hers. He looked back into her mind, searching for her weaknesses as well.

In his mind's eye, Dean glimpsed Lenora Blevins's face, a smiling mother as she sang to her two boys…then her face shifted into a wretched hag with solid-white eyes. Dean somehow knew that she, *it*, was the thing behind all this witchery.

The ancient evil spirit had answered Lenora's conjuring spell and dug its way up from some mold-ridden crevice in the earth. It drew power from women's rage and sorrows, and knew how to manipulate the evil of bad men.

Dean felt the witch-beast burrowing deeper into his mind, searching for all the bad things he'd done. It showed him memories long forgotten—Dean, ten years old, punching a girl in the face, causing her nose to bleed… yelling back at his mother as a teen, smashing one of her favorite china dishes against the wall…cheating on his first girlfriend in college, dumping her for her best friend… all the times he'd watched porn, fantasized about rape, bondage, and whipping women. Dark thoughts that came and went. He knew in his heart he would never rape or harm a woman. But the witch kept showing him a montage of his ugliest thoughts and behaviors. The twisted secrets he never wanted anyone to know.

And she was sending those visions to Sarah, bringing up her darkest fears.

I'm not a monster, Dean wanted to tell her. The witch heightened his senses, made him listen to Sarah crying tears from generations of women's suffering. Made him feel the anguish of all women, witness the countless brutalities that men had done to witches over the centuries—rapes, beatings, murders, burnings. As images of each atrocity passed through his mind, Dean saw his own face on the man committing the violence.

"Get the fuck out of my head!" He walked to the stone wall that was lit up with pagan symbols. With the blunt end of his hatchet-hammer, he pounded the bricks, knocking them loose. He went down the row, chipping the stones, mutilating one hieroglyph after another.

Somewhere in the house the witch-beast howled.

The remaining symbols in the rock walls dimmed and winked out. Dean felt the creature's feelers release from his mind, and the connection between them severed.

The house went silent.

Dean collapsed against the wall, exhausted on every level. But there was no time to rest. While the old witch had been probing his mind, he had probed hers and sensed she had fears of her own. The only man she couldn't manipulate was a man in love. And Dean had been in love with Sarah Donovan since the day he'd met her.

Now she needed him.

21

Dean came up with a completely fucked-up plan that scared the shit out of him.

He paced the floor. The attic window where he'd busted out the clapboards was wide open. He had plenty of rope and climbing gear. He could easily abseil down the steep rock wall and be out of this house. *Go for help,* urged the voice that wanted to increase his odds at living. *Bring the police.*

But in the time that would take, Sarah would be dead, if she wasn't already. No, she was still alive. He had to believe that. He couldn't let doubt destroy his will. *You brought Sarah in here, Dean—now do whatever it takes to bring her out.*

Back to Plan A.

He shut out all the voices driven by fear and got busy. He slipped his knife back into its sheath and kept the hatchet handy. He checked his backpack. Among climbing tools, he had some extra rope, first-aid kit, bottled water, snack bars and three red flares. "Bingo." He opened the medical kit and saw he had a bottle of rubbing alcohol. "Double bingo."

Outside the open window, the sky turned charcoal

gray. His ally, the sun, had abandoned him and descended behind the tops of the pine trees. The light near the window retreated and the darkness began to claim the attic once more.

He took a deep breath to calm his nerves. His fear was heightened by a surge of adrenaline. The same rush he felt when he was about to climb the face of a steep mountain. He poured climber's chalk on his sweaty hands then slipped his fingerless gloves back on.

He started back through the maze of crates and antiques. The plastic draping fluttered upward as he passed. He panned his flashlight left and right, wary there might be mold people hiding, but none attacked. When the light from the engraved stones died out, the ghosts must have returned to being fungus on the walls.

Dean reached the attic's door and tested the knob. Still locked. "Damn it." He remembered the box of old tools he'd found earlier. If he could find a small screwdriver he might be able to take the knob off. He looked back at the clutter of heirlooms, trying to recall where the toolbox had been.

"Ah, screw it!" He turned around and began chopping at the door. It split down the center. He was making a hell of a racket. No covert operation, this plan. It took multiple blows from his hatchet to rend a crack large enough to slip his arm through. He felt for a latch on the other side. No such luck. Just a keyhole.

Dean got a sudden fear that the witch was just beyond the door and he backed away. He jabbed his light beam through the crack. The top of the stairwell was empty. Where was the old hag? He imagined her down in the cellar, drinking Sarah's blood like a vampire. This fueled his anger. He kept chopping and chopping until the door split in half. He tossed the broken pieces aside. Adrenaline pumping, he almost charged down the stairs, but his instincts stopped him. The enclosed staircase turned halfway down. The witch could be crouched around the corner, waiting for him to come down. The stairwell was so narrow Dean wouldn't be able to move his arms to fight her.

Scratch Plan A—move to Plan B.

Maybe he could draw the witch up here.

He walked back through the storage area to the opposite side where there was more space to maneuver. Taking a deep breath, he lit one of the red flares and gripped the handle of the hatchet-hammer.

Okay, Dean, let's do this.

He hammered the wall, crushing the bricks. "I'm up here! Come after me!"

The witch shrieked. Terrifyingly close.

Dean whipped around, aiming his light at the hole in the broken floor.

22

Ronnie sat on the hood of his truck and lit up another cigarette. He always chain-smoked when he got excited. The Old Blevins House was making all kinds of noise tonight as the predator hunted her prey. With each scream, Ronnie laughed and stomped his boots on the truck's bumper. "Sooooieeee!"

Hot damn how he wished he could be in the house right now, watching Mama take down the piggies. But he didn't trust her when her hunger got this ferocious. So he stayed outside and listened. Sometimes she gave him glimpses of what was happening. He had cheered as the piggy who had hit him with a hammer was carried down to the cellar.

Now Mama was going after the one up in the attic. What a fool that jackass had been to trust Ronnie so easily. Dean had responded to the bogus website offering tours of abandoned haunted houses in East Texas. Ronnie was amazed how many people fell for it. The city folk could be so gullible. He loved it when they brought pretty women. Usually he got to hog-fuck them, but Mama was in a foul mood tonight.

Behind Ronnie, footsteps crunched twigs on the dirt driveway. He turned around to see Otis approaching with his shotgun aimed. He was shaking so badly he could barely hold the barrel straight.

Ronnie smiled at his older brother. "Bubba, it's 'bout time you got here. Mama's show is just getting to the good part." He patted the hood. "Come sit next to me. We'll watch it together."

"No, I won't." Otis shook his head. His bottom lip quivered, and a string of drool fell to his chin. "This…this ain't right."

"Sure it is. I'm just feeding her pigs like you taught me."

"They ain't pigs, Ronnie. They're people."

"You know this is the kind of meat Mama likes best. She's been asking you to bring it for years, hasn't she?"

From the third floor above, the male piggy started yelling and hammering. Then Mama unleashed a roar that sounded like something from hell.

Ronnie stomped his boots again, feeling giddy.

Otis raised his shotgun. "I'm going in and putting a stop to this." He walked to the front door. "What's this?" He yanked at the new padlock.

"The old one was rusty."

"Give me the key."

Ronnie shook his head. "Nope. Not till she's finished."

Otis aimed his barrel at the lock.

"I wouldn't do that if I were you," Ronnie warned.

"Why not?"

"Because if you shoot the lock, you idiot, you're going blow a hole through the door. And when you hurt the house, you hurt Mama. You don't want to hurt Mama, do ya?"

While Otis's imbecile mind tried to process the question, Ronnie said, "Hey, lookie what I got." He raised a bottle of Southern Comfort and took a swig.

Otis licked his lips, his eyes now transfixed on the bottle. He had a weakness for whiskey. Whenever Ronnie wanted to take his prey to the house, he'd get his brother drunk until he passed out. Otis could sleep for two days on a good bender.

Ronnie guzzled another swig and wiped his mouth. "Ahhhh. You can have some, if you'll come over here."

Otis shook his head. "Give me the key or I swear I'll…" He walked toward Ronnie.

Ronnie stood on the hood of his truck and held the key high over Otis's head.

He jumped up for it, clawing the air. "Give it to me, damn it!"

"Gotta catch me first." Ronnie hopped to the ground, jangling the keys, and ran around the side of the house. Hooting and laughing, he looked back to see the fool chasing after him, too stupid to realize the man with the gun usually had the upper hand.

23

Holding his breath, Dean watched the hole in the attic floor. He expected Lenora Blevins to climb up the rope, poking her hag face above the edge. He imagined her short and decrepit, but made strong and agile from black magic. The thought of fighting a woman sickened him. No, she was not a woman, but some undead thing that had clawed its way up from hell. This beast had murdered his friends and intended to kill him and Sarah.

Gripping the hatchet and a burning flare in his fists, Dean was prepared to fight to the death. "Come up here and get me, you old bitch!"

The floorboards beneath his feet began to buckle. Nails shot upward. Wood cracked. The dark hole widened, the boards caving in. Dean dove as the floor dropped beneath him. He landed on solid planks. Not looking back, he crawled to the storage area, hid behind a dresser. He aimed his light beam at the rectangular gulch that now spanned the width of the attic.

Down below, boards crashing on the second floor finally settled. Then silence.

Dust floated in the air as his light passed over the abyss. Where was she?

He heard scraping and chittering. Then black roots shot upward from the breach like kraken tentacles and whipped the air. One picked up a lamp near Dean's head and shattered it against the rafters. The appendages twined around the crossbeams and pulled up a writhing black mass through the gap.

Dean raced through the maze of antiques.

The creature shrieked behind him. It tore through the stored boxes and furniture, smashing everything in its path. A long arm flew past Dean and knocked over a grandfather clock.

"Shit!" He ran for the stairwell. As he reached the exit, a wooden tentacle wrapped around his ankle, yanked him off his feet. Dragged him on his stomach. It slammed him against a wall, bruising his shoulder. Growling in anger, Dean grabbed the long root, which squirmed like a snake in his hand, and chopped it with his hatchet. Blood poured out from the severed ends.

The witch-beast cried out in pain.

Her massive body rose to the ceiling, towering over him. His light shined upon a mottled black torso of undulating skin covered in roots and crawling insects. From its sides moved multiple arms and swooping feelers. Several of them clung to the rafters, as its twitching body hung from the ceiling. The flesh opened up in its belly. From two slits emerged hands with claws that stretched toward Dean. He bolted to the stairwell and raced down the steps.

The beast screeched and chased after him, thundering across the floorboards.

As he turned the corner, wooden tentacles speared into the wall behind him. Dean hurried down the stairs. More feelers snaked after him. A cord wrapped around his waist, pulling him upward.

He slammed the hatchet into the wall and clung to the handle. In his other hand, he held onto the burning flare, and turned, ready to fight.

Up the stairwell, a Hydra of fleshy stalks and rootlike vines slapped the walls and ceiling. Two twined around his ankles, lifting Dean off his feet. Suspended in midair, they opened his legs wide. He yelled and struggled to break loose. A long arm swung around the corner, its claw-tipped hand reaching for his crotch. In the center of the palm an eyeball glared.

The witch cackled from the attic.

"Fuck you!" Dean pressed the flare against the hand's eye, scorching it until the orb popped.

The witch-beast wailed.

While she was distracted by pain, Dean singed every tentacle he could reach, catching the tips on fire. The vines released him and slithered back up the stairwell and around the corner.

Dean stumbled down the final stairs to the second-floor hallway, collapsed to his knees. He heard the beast thrashing above. Prayed it had caught fire and was dying. The thumps and clattering and cries of pain moved farther and farther away.

Shit, it's on the move.

He had to find Sarah. He retrieved his hatchet, lit up a second flare, and pulled out his secret weapon. Then he sprinted down the hallway, praying he reached the cellar first.

24

Sarah woke up in a black void that smelled of moist soil and something rotting. A critter with spidery legs crawled across her cheek. She tried to brush it off, but her arm was stuck. Her face was free to breathe, but the rest of her head and body had been buried in a shallow grave. She felt worms squirming against her arms and legs. Claustrophobia took over and panic followed. She rocked back and forth, hyperventilating. Her thrashing loosened the soil, creating small pockets between her body and the wormy grave walls. One arm broke free. She clawed at the damp earth and dug out her other arm. Sarah sat up and dirt crumbled down her chest, into her shirt and bra. She slapped at insects crawling on her face and arms. Unburying her legs, she dragged herself out. She tried to stand and hit her helmet on a low ceiling.

Where the hell am I? She switched on her helmet lamp. She caught glimpses of cave walls, dangling roots. The beam flickered, went out. The darkness closed around her.

"Come on. Come on." She slapped her helmet and the light came back on, throwing a spotlight on a black-stained rock ceiling. She backed away from the dripping fungus and hit something that rattled. Twisting around, she saw human skeletons embedded in the earth walls like fossils.

Sarah screamed as she realized she had been buried in a mass grave. *The bodies of the witches had never been found,* Ronnie had said.

Frantic, she crawled away and found a tunnel that sloped upward. The rock-and-root ceiling was too low for her to stand. Her hands and knees sank in the soil as she wormed her way upward. She spat grit from her mouth. She grabbed roots to pull herself up. At the top, Sarah birthed herself from the earthen womb, only to find herself in the cellar. Behind her were shelves lined with jars of pus-gray liquid and molded mush. The sealed Mason jars were labeled—*Apples, Peaches, Strawberry Jam, Pickled Pigs' Feet.* Smelling a fermented stench, she put a hand across her mouth and nose, trying not to vomit.

Beneath the shelves was a burrow that looked like something a giant badger might have dug. The tunnel to the mass grave must have sloped thirty feet under the house. The creature's lair.

Sarah stood and hurried along the foundation's stone wall, hoping it led to an exit. The pitch-dark within the cellar seemed to go on forever. She feared any moment the ghost witches would see her light and attack her, then bury her alive again in the burrow, deeper this time. But the thought of shutting off her light and walking blind terrified her even more.

She listened but nothing moved down here but insects and occasional drips. As she ventured farther, she began to hear a distant voice coming from somewhere straight ahead. *Please be Dean.* In a vision, she'd seen him hanging in the attic, but she wasn't willing to believe he was dead.

She clung to the hope that they would find each other and somehow escape this house.

Her hiking shoes crunched something—a human skull submerged in the soil. Panning her light, she saw several bone fragments scattered across the dirt floor. One of them was a whole rib cage that still had bits of pink meat on it. It was covered in beetles.

Reaching a corner, she gasped at the sight of Meg's and Casey's severed heads impaled on pikes. Their mouths hung open, eye sockets hollow. All around them dozens of other skulls were perched on sticks.

Sarah teared up and hurried past the creature's trophies, feeling heartbroken and terrified for her own life. She didn't want to end up like all the victims before her.

Up ahead, Sarah saw the faintest pale light. It illuminated a large hole in the cellar wall. She probed her light beam into a tunnel that stretched for about twenty feet. At the other end—moonlight. Her heart surged. A way out. She ran through the tunnel, passing animal carcasses and pig skulls that had been picked clean. The passage ended at a circular rock wall and went straight upward—the well shaft she had nearly fallen into earlier that day. The water was only a few inches deep. Looking up she saw steep rock walls and the full moon in a dark-gray sky. The climb looked impossible without rope and Dean to belay her.

Sarah fell back against the rock and started to cry. Her death would be one of irony now, having come so close to escaping. Soon her head would find its place among the impaled skulls and her body would fossilize the walls where the creature fed and slept.

She heard someone talking and moving around up

there. She backed into the tunnel, afraid it was Ronnie.

Then the man's voice became clearer. He had a deeper voice than Ronnie's.

Feeling a burst of hope, Sarah rushed back into the moonlight. "Hello? Is anyone up there? I need help! Please help!" She made as much noise as she could.

A man's bald silhouette peered over the top of the hole. He was holding a gun. He shined a light in her eyes. "You're still alive," he said. "I could've sworn you'd be dead by now."

Oh God, another killer like Ronnie, she thought as the man stared at her. Having no other choice, she decided to gamble. "Please, help me out of here!"

He took several long seconds to think about this, shaking his head. "Mama's not gonna like it. Not one bit. She's gonna be madder than the devil at me."

"Please…" Sarah begged. "There's something in the house killing people." She cried with desperation.

The man held up his palm. "All right, hold on, miss, we'll get you out. Watch your head." He dropped a chain down that clinked at her feet. "Tie that around your waist and I'll pull you up."

As Sarah grabbed the chain, she heard Dean calling her name from somewhere in the cellar. "Wait, I hear Dean!" she yelled up to the man. "Please, wait!"

She ran back down the tunnel, yelling Dean's name. He called back to her, sounding so far away. Tears of relief poured from Sarah's eyes. *He's alive!* When she reached the cellar, her beam lit up a black torso with multiple arms. Sarah screamed as tentacles wrapped around her and pulled her into the darkness.

25

"No, Mama!" Otis yelled into the well shaft, when he saw in his head the girl had been snatched away.

He was so afraid for her, he was shaking all over.

He could feel that Mama was in pain now and full of fury. His own hand hurt where she had been burned by the man in the attic. Now she aimed to rip the girl apart and then the man, limb by limb, before drinking them dry.

"Please don't hurt them, Mama!" his voice echoed. "I'll bring you a pig tonight if you're still hungry."

Ronnie yelled from the dark woods. "She's already got her pigs, you idiot."

Otis walked to the edge of the backyard, searching for where Ronnie was hiding.

"Damn it, bring me the keys! I need to help them."

"Here then." The keys flung through the air and landed in the high grass.

As Otis bent over and started searching the grass, Ronnie tackled him, slamming him against the ground. Otis felt several punches to the face. Then everything went dark.

* * *

Ronnie whistled as he dragged Otis across the grass and laid his limp body in a patch of moonlight. "Damn retard." Ronnie kicked his brother's ribs, but Otis didn't so much as jerk. Ronnie wrapped the chain around Otis's ankles, then stepped up to the hole.

He rattled the chain against the walls of the well shaft. "Mama, I got some more meat up here. Come and get it."

The chain didn't move. He heard screams below and realized Mama was already feeding.

"Sooie!" Ronnie scooped up the shotgun and took a seat in an old rocking chair. He'd sat here many times, watching piggies screaming as Mama dragged them by the chain into the well. The shaft was such a long drop, they were always unconscious or dead when they hit the bottom. The really fun ones, though, were the piggies he locked inside the house.

Drinking from his whiskey bottle, Ronnie regretted not bringing a bag of popcorn as he closed his eyes and watched the show Mama played inside his head.

26

Dean's headlamp beam and two glowing red flares carved a swath through the black void inside the cellar. "Sarah!" He had heard her calling his name and then she'd gone silent. He kept yelling for her, wary the noise might draw the witch-beast to him. He didn't care. He'd face it again if it meant saving Sarah.

Above ground, the house was extremely wide with long corridors. Down here, the windowless cellar seemed to span the full length and width of the house. A cavern of infinite darkness, moldy ceiling and black soil. The farther Dean walked toward the back, the ranker it smelled. Like road kill. He saw a backlit circle up ahead. A giant hole in the wall tunneled out to a moonlit exit.

Had Sarah escaped?

Dean quickened his steps. His boots crunched over bones and bloody clothing. The witch-beast's feeding ground. He saw the collection of skulls on sticks and grimaced at the sight of Meg's and Casey's heads. No time to mourn them. Dean was too full of fight-or-flight adrenaline right now.

Twenty feet ahead, Sarah's headlamp switched on. She stood there waving frantically, with an odd smile on her face. She spun, doing a pirouette like a ballerina, and then her light turned off.

"Sarah!" He marched toward her. "Where are you?"

She didn't respond.

Hearing a chittering noise, he stopped and spun around. His light found a pair of shoes, Sarah's feet floating inches above the dirt. As he panned his light up her body to her face, he saw cords wrapped around her legs and torso and a bony black hand covering her mouth. Sarah's eyes were wide with terror.

The witch-beast pulled her into the blackness.

"Come back here!" Double-fisting the flares, Dean advanced. He heard a yelp and tossed a flare in that direction. The red glow lit up the multilimbed creature and all its ugliness. The vines swooped around its body. At the center of its torso was Lenora Blevins's hag face with two solid-white eyes. Her head stretched outward on a thick, fleshy stalk. A mouth with gray gums and sharp wooden teeth came straight for Dean. He backpedaled, holding out the flare.

The witch-beast's floating head reared away from the flame and shrieked like a banshee.

It tossed Sarah to the ground and charged.

"Dean!" Sarah cried.

"Run to the tunnel!" He drew the beast away from her. Its root tentacles snaked across the ceiling. One curled around his arm. He severed it with the hatchet. He walked backwards in an arc, trying to move the creature in a circle. Instead of following, it countered his move, keeping Dean from getting around it. An arm lashed out and struck his chest. He rolled across the dirt, feeling a fiery pain. Across his chest and shoulder were five gashes. Blood seeped through his shirt.

As the predator came in for the kill, Dean saw the other red flare approaching from behind the beast. Sarah attacked its blind side, torching its vines.

"No, Sarah! Run!"

The creature spun, its head-on-a-stalk whipping around and roaring at Sarah. The vines wrapped around her, lifting her in the air.

Dean jumped to his feet, ran screaming with the hatchet held above his head and leaped onto the beast's back. He chopped into its flesh, breaking wooden bones and severing vines.

The hag's head wailed. Its stalk neck curled back around its body. Dean, still on its back, swung the blade and lopped off its head. The bleeding stump whipped through the air, spraying black ooze across the ceiling. The witch-beast's body fell to the ground, convulsing.

Dean hopped down and ran to Sarah.

She threw her arms around his waist. "Thank God."

He touched her face. "Are you okay?"

She nodded. Her face was filthy and streaked with tears, but she was alive.

She saw the gash in his shoulder. "You're bleeding."

"It's nothing."

They both looked at the massive thing flopping on the ground, its roots and vines digging into the soil around it. The fleshy stalk that had been its neck was now limp and gushing out black blood. Lenora's severed hag's head sat in the soil, gaping at them with lifeless white eyes.

"Please get me out of this house," Sarah said.

As they walked around the writhing body of the beast, Dean noticed all its roots had stabbed into the soil and were shaking as if they were drinking the earth.

In a sudden blur, the creature rose to the ceiling. In its mottled black torso, what looked like a dozen female faces buried in tar pressed the gelatinous skin outward. Slits opened. Two more heads shot out on stalks. One face looked like Lenora, the other an even older hag-creature.

Dean pushed Sarah to move. "Run!"

As she sprinted ahead of him down the tunnel, Dean watched in horror as the witch-beast sprouted new limbs and roots. He had lost his hatchet. He was down to one flare and a bottle of rubbing alcohol, and this beast didn't seem to die. He bolted into the tunnel, racing toward the moonlit hole at the other end. Sarah was already there, climbing up a chain.

The witch-beast's enormous body squeezed into the passage, roaring. Dean ran backwards, keeping the two chomping heads at bay with his flare stick. He reached the well shaft, backed against the rock wall.

The creature's thick torso got stuck near the edge of the tunnel, but the two floating hag heads kept barreling toward him. As they entered the well shaft, Dean threw the alcohol into their faces. He torched Lenora's head with the flare's fiery tip; then he jammed the flare into the cheek of the older hag. Both heads caught fire and shrieked in pain.

The witch-beast retreated, her two burning heads floating backward to the cellar.

27

While Dean fought back the beast, Sarah wrapped the chain around her waist and climbed ten feet up the wall. Then her fear of heights kicked in. She clung to the rock, afraid of falling. Dean scaled the rock with just as much difficulty. His shoulder was bleeding badly and he looked like he was getting weaker. "We have to keep climbing. She's not dead."

Sarah could hear the beast wailing inside the tunnel.

The climb to the top of the shaft looked menacing. Sarah rattled the chain and yelled for the man who had dropped it down to her, but he didn't respond.

Dean touched her arm. "You can do this. There are plenty of footholds and places to grip. Just reach up and find a grip, then push up with your legs and feel for the next ledge to place your foot. Always keep your eyes on the rocks right above you." He guided her upward, coaching her the whole way.

Sarah began to find the juts and crags on her own. Her feet found purchase on thin ledges and pushed her body upward. Her muscles strained. She slipped once, but Dean caught her arm and helped her regain her grip of the wall. Sarah moved faster.

Dean fell behind. His face had turned pasty. He groaned every time he reached up with his right arm.

"Keep coming, Dean," she encouraged.

"Don't wait on me. Go on up."

"No, we're sticking together every step of the way."

Sarah heard the *clink* of metal up above. The chain around her waist snapped taut and she felt herself being pulled upward.

"Dean!" She reached for his hand, but only grazed his fingers as the chain pulled her away from him. She heard the *clacking* of the pulley above. Had the bald man returned?

When she reached the top, the chain stopped moving, and she remained suspended over the hole. Dean was still halfway down.

"Keep climbing, Dean." She grabbed a tuft of grass and pulled herself to the edge, thankful to see the outside world again.

Ronnie approached, holding a shotgun. "Well, lookie here, if it isn't Miss Piggy." He pushed a boot against her shoulder, causing her to spin over the hole. "It ain't polite to leave in the middle of supper."

"Ronnie, don't you hurt her!" Dean yelled from below.

"I'm not gonna hurt her. I'm gonna hog-fuck her right here while you watch." He aimed the shotgun. "And don't think of trying to climb up or I'll blow your fucking head off." He fired a shot at the sky. "Don't think I won't."

Sarah felt Ronnie's hand grab her belt and pull her onto the grass. He unraveled the chain from her waist. Forced her onto her hands and knees and positioned her at the edge of the well. She could see Dean inching his way up.

After all the two of them had been through, Sarah's body filled with anger toward this backwoods lunatic. She jerked her wrist when Ronnie groped her breast.

He grabbed a snatch of her hair and pulled her head back. "Now, you better not get feisty, or I'm gonna throw you back in the hole."

"Just get it over with." She stopped resisting and pretended to surrender, while in her mind, she frantically searched for a way out of this.

Ronnie got behind her, slapped her backside. "Sooie, what a night! You and I are gonna have some fun."

The she-beast screeched at the bottom of the shaft.

"Wait your turn, Mama. You can have her when I'm done." He set the shotgun on the ground, unzipped his pants, and pulled them down.

Sarah dug her nails into the grass. Gritted her teeth.

As Ronnie hugged her from behind and unbuckled her shorts, she elbowed him in the jaw. Something channeled through her—the rage of his mama or Sarah's own—but she was suddenly a feral beast.

She spun and clawed at Ronnie's face, gouged his eyes.

He screamed in pain as Sarah bit down on his right ear and ripped the flesh loose. Blood spurted down his neck. But Sarah's hunger for vengeance didn't stop there. She grabbed his testicles and squeezed until they burst in her hands.

Ronnie cried out. He grabbed his bleeding groin and squirmed on the ground.

Sarah reached for the shotgun but it was gone. She turned around and saw a buck-toothed man was holding it. She froze. He held Sarah's gaze for a long moment and she feared he was going to shoot her.

The witch-beast yelled from the shaft, "Feed them to me, Otie!"

The man in overalls ran a hand across his dim-witted face. "No, Mama, I won't do it. They never done nothing to us."

Otis walked over to Ronnie, who wouldn't stop screaming, and clubbed him with the butt of the shotgun.

Ronnie fell silent.

Dean climbed over the edge of the hole and Sarah ran to him. As he stood, she hugged him close and tight.

Otis pointed the gun at them and said, "Get out of here! Go on!"

28

An hour later, Otis sat in his rocker in the backyard, drinking whiskey and looking up at the full moon. Rocking and drinking.

On the ground, his wounded younger brother stirred and lifted his blood-covered face. Ronnie was blind now, his eyes pressed too far back into his head. All Otis could see were the whites of the eyeballs and bloody tears. One ear was missing and the jeans at Ronnie's crotch were soaked red. A real mess, he was.

He cried and moaned until Otis couldn't take no more.

Sometimes a pig had to be put out of its misery. And normally Otis had mercy on the swine he had to put down. But tonight there'd be no mercy. Otis walked over to the chain that was wrapped around his brother's waist and jangled it against the rock walls.

Down below, Mama roared with a ferocious hunger that would never end.

Ronnie cried out as he was dragged down into the hole.

29

Sarah drove the white Range Rover down the road, the headlights carving the way through the pines. She kept one hand on the wheel and held Dean's hand with the other. He slept with his head against the window, passed out from exhaustion. Sarah had bandaged his shoulder wound with some gauze she'd found in his first-aid kit. He'd lost a lot of blood, but at least she'd stopped the bleeding.

She prayed she would find a hospital in time. "Hold on, Dean."

As Sarah sped along this road of endless trees, she felt a strange power resonating in her bones and tingling in her palms. It had swept through her when she was with the witch inside the cellar. Lenora Ravenmoon Blevins had appeared from the darkness, smiling with those wild eyes, and gripped Sarah's wrists. "Girl, you have witch's blood in you. Join my coven and together we will have such great power."

Sarah had been too terrified to respond.

"Here is just a taste." Lenora had filled Sarah with power until she shook, and with it channeled her rage and thirst for vengeance. The witch's power had unleashed from Sarah when she attacked Ronnie like a wild animal.

Somehow she knew it wasn't just her anger, but the fury of his mother. No one hurt her dear sweet Otis, the only person she ever loved.

Now Sarah looked into the rearview mirror and saw her eyes had darkened. She still felt a connection with not only the witch that lived in the cellar, but the long lineage of witches who had discovered the benefits of magick.

Sarah's grandmother suddenly spoke inside her head, *You can keep receiving this power, and no man who tries to harm you will ever stand a chance against you. You can magically heal Dean; make him stay in love with you; create a family with him. All you have to do is join the coven and accept the magick that is your birthright.*

Sarah became confused. Nana had always taught that White Magic was light and used to improve one's life. And Black Magic and conjuring evil spirits always came with a high price.

Remember the rule of three, her grandmother had preached. *Whatever you send out into the world, good or bad, will come back to you threefold.* Her grandmother would never use a spell on a man to control him.

Lenora's mimicking Nana to seduce me. Sarah looked into the rearview mirror again and saw Lenora's eyes staring back. *Come back to me.*

Sarah felt the sudden urge to turn the car around, but fought it. "No, never. I denounce your offer. Now, get the hell out of my head!"

In the mirror Lenora's eyes burned with rage and the glass cracked.

Immediately, Sarah felt the witch's hold rip loose. The darkness left Sarah's eyes. Her palms stopped tingling and the energy surge in her body drained until all she felt was tired from everything that had happened.

Sarah squeezed Dean's hand and imagined sending all her love into him. What her grandmother would call "white magick" that naturally flowed from a loving heart.

Dean woke up as if pulled out of a bad dream. He turned to her. Their eyes gazed into one another's, and the connection between them was so much stronger than the power she had felt from the cellar witch's magick.

His hand squeezed hers, and a new, deeper love for this man expanded inside her body. With Dean at her side, Sarah knew they could conquer anything in this world, and beyond.

Epilogue

At midnight, Otis was walking through the house when sirens wailed from up the road. He figured that young couple notified the authorities. It was just as well. Otis was getting too old and was tired of being the house's caretaker. The Blevins family bloodshed had gone on too long, and it would end with him.

He made his way down to the cellar. Waiting for him in the darkness was the giant monstrosity that Mama had grown into. Her wounds looked healed after eating a fresh meal and drinking from the soil. She stood next to a large burrow.

As Otis approached, the wet flesh from the creature's torso split and opened up like wings. Beneath the thin, membraned tissue of its interior, he saw the outline of Lenora Blevins, the way his mama looked before she had changed.

She smiled through the skin veil and opened her arms. "It's time to go to our secret hidey-hole, Little Otie."

"I'm ready, Mama." Otis embraced her, crying joyful tears on her bosom, as the flesh of the beast cocooned around them and took them down into the earth.

# # #

Some people are haunted by demons.

An emotionally scarred poet, Marty Weaver, has been bullied his whole life. Three sadistic killers think he's the perfect victim to star in their snuff film. But when the killers trigger Marty's buried pain and rage—and unleash his vengeful demon—blood will flow and hell will rise.

"Moreland has assembled a masterpiece novella that I cannot recommend enough. Upon first reading, this is easily one of my favorite horror releases of the year."
–Horror Underground

"Horror fans will find plenty of chills."
–The Horror Maiden

Beneath the city of Boston, evil is gathering.

While living under a bridge with the homeless for six months, journalist Daniel Finley witnessed something terrifying. Something that nearly cost him his sanity.

Now, two years later, he's published a book that exposes a deadly underground cult and its charismatic leader who preaches a dark prophecy. Down in the abandoned subway tunnels exist unimaginable horrors. And in a church of darkness, the cult's numbers are growing. Soon Daniel's worst nightmares are coming true. A fanatical army is rising to shed blood on the streets of Boston.

"Chocked full of scares and suspense…
This is the kind of story horror lovers need."
–Kristopher Rufty, author of *The Lurkers*

A vacation in tropical paradise turns to terror.

When four tourists leave their boat to explore an isolated island in the Philippines, their daytrip spirals into a nightmare. This island conceals dark secrets: deadly inhabitants lurk in the overgrown jungle. Ravenous and bloodthirsty, they prey upon unfortunate visitors who dare to venture into the jungle.

"A fast-paced and very entertaining read, Brian Moreland's latest novella, *Savage Island*, delivers in buckets and spades..."
–Horror DNA

About the Author

Brian Moreland writes dark suspense, thrillers, and horror. His books include *Shadows in the Mist, The Devil's Woods, The Witching House, The Seekers, Darkness Rising, Savage Island, Tomb of Gods* and *They Stalk the Night*. His short stories have appeared in several horror anthologies.

An adventure seeker and world traveler, Brian has visited over twenty countries. He enjoys hiking, caving, and exploring new places. He currently lives in North Texas, where he is writing scary books and short stories.

Follow on Twitter/X: @BrianMoreland

Printed in Dunstable, United Kingdom

71038795R00092